Emerson Dunn Mysteries
by Roy Maynard

.38 Caliber
.22 Automatic

(more to come)

22 AUTOMATIC

AN EMERSON DUNN MYSTERY

Roy Maynard

CROSSWAY BOOKS • WHEATON, ILLINOIS
A DIVISION OF GOOD NEWS PUBLISHERS

.22 Automatic.

Published by Crossway Books, a division of
Good News Publishers, 1300 Crescent Street, Wheaton, Illinois 60187.

Cover illustration: Keith Stubblefield

Art Direction/Design: Mark Schramm

First printing, 1993

Printed in the United States of America

Library of Congress Cataloging-in-Publication Data
Maynard, Roy.
   .22 Automatic : an Emerson Dunn mystery / Roy Maynard.
     p.   cm.
   I. Title.   II. Title: Twenty-two caliber.
PS3563.A96387A613 1993   813'.54—dc20   92-21559
ISBN 0-89107-696-4

01		00		99		98		97		96		95		94		93
15	14	13	12	11	10	9	8	7	6	5	4	3	2	1

To the Pearsons:
Calvin, Jan, Anna,
John, and Deborah;
to Yossi, and as always,
to Sara

1

Somewhere a saxophone was playing soft and slow.
I couldn't hear it, but I knew it had to be out there some-where. A saxophone is always playing soft and slow when a drop-dead gorgeous blonde walks into your office on a tired evening. I know — I've seen all the old movies. And just like in those movies, her eyes are bound to distract you from the fact that she's about to land you in a world of trouble. That's how this sort of story always begins.

She was dressed in a conservative gray business suit, an ivory blouse, black hose, black pumps, and red lipstick — lipstick the subtle shade of a stop sign. I should have taken the stop sign hint. Instead, I took the envelope she handed me wordlessly. Probably not the best move I've ever made, but we'll get to that part later.

It was a bit of an effort to take my eyes off of her and look at the envelope. It was sealed, and it had one word written on it: Emerson.

That's me — Emerson Dunn. I thought I recognized the hand-writing, but I was certain I didn't recognize the blonde. Not even from any of the old movies. I took a letter opener from my desk drawer and opened the envelope. Inside was a single page — a handwritten note to me.

Emerson,

Remember that favor you owe me? Here's your big chance. Do what Meagan asks. I told her she could trust you. My love to Remington and David.

Sally Nix

P.S. Please try to play fair.

I looked back up at the blonde.

"OK, I give up," I said. "What is it you two want me to do?"

"Nothing much," she said. "Just check me out."

She pulled a sheet of paper from a briefcase I hadn't noticed she was carrying. She handed it to me. It was a resumé with a name, a date of birth, and some jobs and duties and dates listed.

"Are you looking for a job?"

"Yes, but not here," she said. "This is a trial run. Sally said you'd help. All you have to do is pretend you're an employer with an opening in your sales department. Pretend I came in and gave you that resumé. Check me out, then tell me if you'd hire me. If you wouldn't, tell me why. Do you have time for this?"

"Well, free time is about the only thing I have plenty of lately," I said. "I'm not doing much around here."

I looked around the empty newspaper office. This late on a Monday night, everyone had gone home. The only reason I was still at my desk was to type up yet another rough draft of the preliminary outline of a novel I had in my head but couldn't seem to get onto paper. I think I knew in the back of my mind that I'd never get it finished; it's the great bane of newshounds that we all have a great novel in our heads but only cheap ink in our veins. The only words we really love are the ones we see on impermanent newsprint the next day. We also have short attention spans. But where was I . . .

I looked back down at the resumé. Her name was Margaret Sullivan. Born in Boston. Just a few years younger than I, but I would have guessed she was older. Margaret Sullivan from Boston . . .

"Maggie?" I asked.

She blushed. I was right. Irish heritage; she was probably in the first or at most second generation of her family to be born in the States. Her father probably spoke with a brogue and called her Wee Maggie ever since her cradle days.

"Who's Meagan?" I asked, looking back at Sally's note.

"Me," she said. "That's the name I once went by."

She offered no more information. She just looked at me.

"Why not hire a private eye?" I asked. "I'm just a reporter. Private investigators do background checks like this all the time."

"Because they have more resources than other people," Meagan or Maggie or Margaret said. "I want you to find out as much as a normal personnel director would — no more, no less. Besides, Sally said you'd do this for free, as a favor to her. If you don't want to, I understand."

"I'll do it," I said after a moment. "Where can I reach you?"

"At the Holiday Inn," she said. "Room 111. Call me when you think you've done as thorough a check as you can. If I don't hear from you within a week, I'll check back."

She smiled at me and left.

For about five minutes I stared at the door. I didn't know whether to thank Sally Nix or hide in my room for a few months.

Sally was a cop I knew. She'd been a key player in breaking the biggest story of my career (to date, that is; let's be optimistic). She was an honest cop, a pretty woman, and she'd proven to be a competent investigator since she'd gotten her promotion.

That story had won me a promotion too, but I wasn't enjoying it. Now that I was the managing editor of the *Times* in this small Texas Gulf Coast town, I spent most of my day watching my new staff covering the kinds of stories I had been having a blast covering six months ago. The girl I dated, A. C. Remington, had helped break that story, too. She'd been working on the other newspaper in town, the *Courier*.

But after The Story, one of the big Houston papers had hired Remington immediately. She was now working in the Pasadena bureau, about an hour's drive from town. We both knew it would be better for her to move to Pasadena, but she said she felt that this was home. I didn't argue. I also didn't get to see her much, despite the fact that she still lived here in town.

I hadn't seen Sally Nix in about six weeks. Last I heard, she was working undercover in Nueces County in some kind of an inter-county cop exchange program.

The problem with small towns in Texas — small towns anywhere, I guess — is that everyone knows you. It's tough to go undercover if you sat through homeroom class with the drug dealer you're hoping to bust. So there's a lot of inter-department cooperation. Sally was over there, and I'd bet that when the bell rang at our high school in the morning, a Nueces County narc would walk into biology class carrying a notebook.

I gave up on the Great American Novel and switched off the computer. I locked the office doors on my way out and climbed into my car, a blue 1973 Ford.

As I started the car, I wondered where to go. It's kind of hard to go somewhere if you don't know where you're going. I looked at my watch; it was just after 8 P.M. Remington would still be in Pasadena at a school board meeting.

The late July heat had started to ease up as the sun started going down. This close to the coast, the muggy heat could get downright depressing. Although it was cooling off, the air still felt hot and sticky.

I pulled out of the parking lot and drove toward home, still thinking about Margaret. The more I thought about her, the less I was sure of. But there was little I could do that night, so I drove through town, crossed the main drag, Commerce Street, and eventually pulled into my driveway.

I looked a couple of driveways down the small street and saw no sign of a green Chevrolet. That meant my landlord wasn't home; he and the suffering saint who married him and put up with him were probably off somewhere spending my rent money. I had gotten a raise with the promotion and was now falling into the bad habit of paying my rent on time. That really threw old Mr. Ewen for a loop; he found almost nothing to grouse about these days. Mrs. Ewen, the wonderful woman who on several occasions prevented her husband from kicking me out, kept telling the old guy, "I told you so. He's a nice boy, that Emerson." I tended to agree with her, of course, but that's just my opinion.

Deep down, I was glad they weren't home. I was putting off what I knew would be a tough task. I had to tell old man Ewen and his wife that I was moving. I'd found a house to rent — a small farmhouse with two bedrooms and about an acre's worth of beautiful yard. The rest of the land that had been the farm was now leased to an absentee rancher who ran cattle on it. Consequently, my closest neighbors were bovines. I didn't mind. The house was just past the west edge of town, down an obscure and unattended farm-to-market road. That meant my commute into work would double from about five minutes to about ten minutes; it also meant I could bring my dog down from my parents' home in Dallas. Airborne Ranger (Airhead, as my dad lovingly referred to him) would enjoy the big backyard and the surrounding fields full of rabbits, mice and squirrels. And cows.

My soon-to-be next-door neighbor (a half-mile away, on the other side of the cows) was a farmer who was getting along in years. His son came out from town every morning to help him put out some feed for the old, lame horse he still had. The plethora of animals might confuse my dog, I realized. I don't think Airborne had ever seen a cow; I wondered if he'd recognize the horse as lunch. As golden retrievers go, Airborne wasn't the most worldly-wise. He'd never actually retrieved anything more menacing than a tennis ball, but nevertheless I had high hopes for our future together in the wilderness.

I walked up the stairs to my current apartment, the top half of a two-story house that Ewen had built just before he was married. He and his wife had raised a family in it; now they'd split it into two apartments, put a kitchen on the top floor, tacked a stairway onto the side leading up to the top floor, and rented it out. It was humble, but it was home. For now.

I walked in, thankful that my air conditioner had been working all day against the Texas heat. I passed through my living room in about three paces and entered my kitchen. The light on my answering machine was blinking, so I hit the Play button.

"Emerson, it's me," came the soft voice of A. C. Remington. "I'm going to be a little late tonight, so I'll just call you at the office tomorrow, OK? Bye."

Touching. We'd been dating since The Big Story, and she'd been helping me teach a junior high Sunday school class every week, but I could feel us growing apart. Maybe it was just the logistics; I had a lot more time these days, and she had a lot less.

The machine beeped once, and a second message played.

"Hey, it's me," said a thick Israeli accent. "I tried you at the office, but you must have left. Call or come over when you get this message. My uncle from Israel is here. I want you to meet him."

I grinned. David Ben Zadok, my photographer and best friend, had told me (warned me, actually) that his Uncle Mordechai was coming into town. I looked at my watch again. It was after 8:30 now, but I knew David and his family wouldn't be the least surprised for me or any other visitor to drop by. I washed up a little and headed back out the door.

David Ben Zadok was about my age, but there the similarities ended.

He'd come to America just more than a year ago to join his mother, who had married an American oil company geologist. Carl Walker, her new husband, had whisked her away to the Land of Opportunity about three years ago and had welcomed her son into their home a couple of years later. Carl was Jewish by heritage and Reformed (fairly liberal in his faith) by nature, but he kept kosher for his new wife, who was Modern Orthodox (what we usually refer to as Conservative Judaism).

In 1981, while still in Israel, David graduated from high school and went straight into the army. Within a few months he was on the front lines of the invasion of Lebanon, commanding a tank.

I figure I was still sitting in English class my senior year when he rolled into Beirut in early June. He spent fourteen months there, then a few more patrolling the Golan Heights. He didn't talk about the war or the army much. After his obligatory three-year stint in the Israeli Defense Forces, he went to school at Tel Aviv University. He spent his spare time shooting free-lance photos for wire services such as AP and Reuters on the West Bank, a short train ride from his dorm room. He often scooped the professionals simply because he paid attention. He knew the codes the army was using, so he'd stand near a jeep and listen to the radio, waiting for the right code words. When a riot would break out, he'd head over to whichever quadrant was heating up and would beat the regular press by as much as half an hour.

Still, Jerusalem is generally not the place where one begins a career in journalism. The best journalists in the world see being sent to Jerusalem as the pinnacle of a career, the top assignment available; so the competition is heavy. David's mother, in love with the Texas coast and her new country, convinced him to come over. He did, carrying two bags. One contained his camera equipment; the other held everything else. David wasn't the kind of guy who lugged around a lot of possessions.

Still thinking about David, I drove through the older part of town until it started turning into the newer part of town. The further from downtown I got, the nicer the homes became. By the time I reached David's street, the houses were neat, brick homes with primped lawns and no plaster lawn statues. I like that in a neighborhood, although I must admit I wouldn't have minded a pink lawn flamingo or two. Nevertheless, I pulled up outside

David's house and parked. I walked up to the door and knocked. David's mother answered almost instantly.

"We're so glad you could come," she said, smiling in a way that absolutely proved she meant it.

Rebecca Ben Zadok Walker was a strong, proud, caring woman. She was dark-haired and olive-skinned, and she carried herself as confidently as her son did.

She took my arm and led me into the dining room. Although it was late there was still food on the table, ready for anyone who might drop in. I recognized some of it; she had pita bread and falafels and some little brown things I'd had before.

Sitting at the table were David, looking stuffed; Carl, looking as if he'd been laughing for hours; and a large man in a dark suit, a hat, a beard, and a prayer shawl. But the black clothes and the prayer shawl expressed joviality more than piety. I looked closely and decided that if Santa Claus had been Jewish, he'd probably look a lot like this guy.

"Emerson, we saved you some," Carl said, looking up at me. Rebecca led me to a seat and was already starting to prepare me a plate full of things that smelled interesting.

David tossed me a yarmulke, and I put it on out of respect. I guessed Mordechai was Orthodox.

"You are David's friend, the one from the newspaper?" boomed Mordechai, the volume of his voice consistent with his girth. His English was passable, his accent strong and pleasant to the ear.

"*Ken*," I said.

"You speak Hebrew?" he asked, lifting an eyebrow.

"Not really. David keeps promising to teach me more, but he never does," I said.

Mordechai sighed.

"I know, I know how David is like. When his mother, my sister, came to America, David lived with me. I tell him every day, 'David, please cut the grass,' and every day he had the same excuse."

Mordechai looked at me somberly and waited. I knew I was being set up.

"OK," I gave in, "what was his excuse?"

"That we lived in apartment on the sixth floor!" Mordechai howled. Carl and David joined him; pretty soon I started laughing too.

Rebecca just shook her head and said something to her brother in Hebrew. David grinned and whispered across the table to me, "She told him that's the third time she's heard this same joke. She told him to get some new ones."

That only made the crowd laugh more. A few moments later I attempted to eat. I wasn't sure I wanted to take my eyes off this bunch. The falafels were still warm, and the brown things turned out to be some kind of peas served chilled. Interesting combination. I kind of liked it. I made a pass at some fish Rebecca had put on my plate.

And then I had tears in my eyes again. The fish was just a bit spicy for me. A bit? I grabbed for a glass of water.

"Watch the fish, Emerson," David warned. "Mordechai cooked tonight. He makes it a little hot."

I nodded and tried to smile.

"No, no, this is not hot," Mordechai protested. "Emerson, you come to Sabbath dinner, I give you hot. I cook then too."

I felt Rebecca's hand on my shoulder.

"Bring A. C., too," she said. "Ruth can't come, and I can't keep my eye on all these men by myself. If I try by myself, they will sneak off and smoke cigars in my house. In my house!"

For the first time, I noticed she was holding an extremely large knife. She started pointing it menacingly at her brother. Obviously she still considered him to be her baby brother and thus in great need of her guidance and gentle discipline.

"You boys don't try it," she said. "Just don't you try it. If I find you with cigars . . ."

Her point was well taken — until she marched out of the room into the kitchen. Then Mordechai, Carl, David and I started howling again with laughter.

The rest of the evening was more of the same. Everything we said was funny, somehow. Rebecca took it like a very vocal martyr, letting us know exactly how much trouble we were and exactly how much suffering she was enduring.

As I stood to leave, I asked Mordechai how long he planned to stay.

"Didn't David tell you? I'm to live here now," he said proudly. "I bought a business. I will sleep on my sister's couch for now, unless she makes me leave because I cook better than she."

More Hebrew denunciations came from the kitchen.

"You will come back for Sabbath dinner?" he asked.

"Sure," I said. "I'd love to."

I called into the kitchen, "Thanks for the meal, Rebecca!"

"You are welcome, you know that," she said, emerging. "And bring A. C. I miss her. I haven't seen her in so long."

You and me both, I thought to myself.

David walked me to the door.

"You like my uncle? He likes you."

"He's great," I said. Then I looked at David's eyes; something was bothering him. I hadn't seen David since last Saturday, because Monday was his usual day off.

"Dave, is something up with Ruth?" I asked, beginning to wonder why David's fiancée wouldn't be occupying her usual spot at the Sabbath dinner table.

"Maybe . . . I don't know. She was supposed to come over tonight, to meet my uncle. She called and said she was busy. She's been busy for a long time."

"I know the feeling," I said. "Remington's the same way. If it weren't for church, I don't think I'd ever see her."

"Women," he said, in that all-encompassing male expression of incomprehension.

"Yeah." But then an unrelated thought occurred to me. "David, you've got to hear about this girl — this woman actually — who walked into the office tonight. Her name is Margaret Sullivan. She's gorgeous. She wanted me to check her job references."

David looked at me and raised his eyebrows.

"She wants a job?"

"No, she just wants me to check on her. Sally Nix sent her to me. She told this girl she could trust me."

David grinned. "That will be the death of you, Emerson. Women feel like they can trust you. And you know what? They can!"

He started laughing again and was soon holding his side and leaning against the door frame. I would have socked him except for three things: 1) He was my best friend, 2) he was right, and 3) he could kill me with his thumbs.

"Tell me how this girl checks out," he said. "I'll see you at work tomorrow."

I left feeling full. I was still a little bothered by the fact that Remington and Ruth seemed too busy for the two great guys they'd landed, but I was getting over it. I put Remington out of my mind and thought about the blonde. I could still picture her; she'd obviously been cultivating that Marilyn Monroe look, with the bleached blonde hair, the way it was cut, and the bright red lipstick. That look somehow didn't mesh with the conservative gray business suit she was wearing.

But so far nothing about her meshed, so why should that surprise me? I knew I couldn't call Sally Nix and ask her about Margaret. Sally was undercover somewhere. All I had to go on was the resumé Margaret had given me — and the insistence of Sally that I "play fair." I guess that meant not talking my cop friend, Detective Sergeant Bill Singer, into running her name through the police computer, then looking the other way as I read the printout. That's not only unfair, it's quite possibly a slight infringement of the law.

As I drove up to my apartment, I realized that my driveway was already occupied. A blue Volvo was sitting in my spot.

Remington's car. I parked on the street and went up the stairs. Remington was inside, doing my dishes. Her back was to me.

"Make yourself at home," I said, probably a little more rudely than I meant. I was glad to see her, but I wasn't going to admit it.

"You didn't lock your door," she said.

"I never do these days. What could happen? Someone could come in and steal my couch? I don't own anything valuable."

She turned around. Aggie Catherine Remington was beautiful, with dark hair and blue eyes you could almost fall into. She looked as if she'd had a rough day; speaking of which, why wasn't she at work?

"Why aren't you at work?" I asked.

"They're getting a little tired of paying me overtime," she said. "And I had three night meetings last week, so I skipped out on the school board tonight. My city editor told me to. So I thought I'd come by here."

The clock on the wall above the sink said 11 P.M.

"How long have you been here?"

"A couple of hours."

"Doing what? My dishes?"

"Look at the rest of the place. Remember, you're the one who picked this month's Sunday school lessons: 'be a servant to others.'"

"Good to see you're paying attention. You're not a bad student."

"You're not a bad teacher. Those kids really like you."

Anna Joyce, the former teacher of the junior high class, was now teaching a "Suddenly Single" class for the women in the small Bible church who had been widowed or divorced. She was doing a great job, but that left me as the permanent teacher for the junior high class. I didn't mind so much; Remington was a big help, and actually I think the kids liked her more than me. They had since the first day I'd brought her with me. The boys thought she was pretty, but she was so old (over twenty!) that the girls didn't feel threatened by her.

"How about some coffee?" she asked.

"I'm out of decaf."

"Not anymore. I also went to the grocery store."

"What is this?" I asked. "You ignore my existence for weeks on end, then you suddenly go off on a Betty Crocker bender. What's the catch?"

Remington looked at me for a moment.

"So it *is* bothering you. I knew it was. You keep telling me it isn't."

Think hard, Dunn, I told myself. *You're a professional with words, so come up with something so witty and disarming she'll completely forget the fact that she's right.*

"So?" I asked. I knew immediately I'd blown it again.

She looked at me with those eyes, demanding more. Time for confession.

"I guess I do miss seeing you; I miss spending as much time with you as I used to spend," I added in sheer, total and utter defeat.

She sat down at the table, across from me.

"Me too." She reached over and took my hand. "Now tell me about the floozy."

2

refuse to reveal my sources," Remington said after I had
unsuccessfully tried to evade the question by asking one of my
own. Kids, don't try this at home. It never works for me, anyway.

It didn't matter. It was a small town; just about anyone driving by could have seen Margaret go in and out of the newspaper
office while my car was the only one still there. I was, in the ver-
nacular, busted.

"Well, she's a friend of Sally's," I said.

"And now she's a friend of yours?"

"Well, no . . . she just came by to ask a favor."

"What kind of favor?"

"She wants me to check on her job references. But she doesn't
want a job."

"Is that all you're going to check out? Should I be checking
your shirts out for bright red lipstick?"

Take me now, O Lord. Just get it over with. Believe me, I didn't
say that out loud.

"Aggie, I'm shocked that you should show such distrust in me.
I'm disappointed in you."

"You'd be more than disappointed, bucko — you'd be maimed
if I really thought I couldn't trust you."

Such a way with words. Such a gentle spirit. I believed her.

"So you do trust me?"

"A little, but don't get overconfident. Now, let's see that resumé."

"I left it at the office."

"Then I guess we won't worry about Miss Blonde Bombshell tonight. Now how about that coffee?"

Remington stayed about another hour; we talked about David and Ruth, among other topics. She told me about her job, what stories she was working on, and about a city council member whom she suspected was about to run for the state legislature.

I told her about the stories being done by Robert and Sherri, the two new reporters I had hired. I also told her how I was getting along with my new publisher, an extremely competent woman named Louise.

Remington lingered a moment before she kissed me good-bye.

"By the way, is there something you're about to forget?" she asked innocently.

Busted again, and this time I didn't even know why. Let's see . . . "Forget," she'd said. That meant I was about to forget our anniversary (nope, we weren't married), the wedding (nope, I hadn't even asked, and neither had she), or her birthday.

Bingo. Her birthday. I'd begun celebration plans a few weeks earlier but then forgot it all. I'm good at that.

"Of course not," I said indignantly. "Would I forget your birthday? Unthinkable."

"Very good," she said, obviously impressed. "So, what do you have in mind?"

OK, now that I knew the exact nature of the threat, I knew how to shore up defenses.

"Dinner — that's all you need to know," I said, adding an air of mystery and buying some time while I was at it. It's good to know how to think on your feet.

"All right," she said. "Dinner Tuesday night."

"Tuesday night. I'll pick you up at 8 P.M."

She kissed me good-bye again and smiled sweetly just before walking out.

Then came her parting shot. "Emerson, my birthday isn't on Tuesday."

Dames.

The next morning it took fifteen minutes of begging to get Detective Sergeant Bill Singer to find out Remington's birthday for me. I was at my desk, and all the while our receptionist Sharon was smirking.

"It's Thursday," Singer said after a moment of effortless computer work. "And you owe me big. You don't even want to *think* about how much you owe me."

"For what? For punching a few letters into the computer? What's the big deal?"

"The big deal is, it's her birthday. You mess that up and you won't be worth sending an ambulance for. If I hadn't found this out for you, we might as well have called out the medical examiner and declared you dead right now; it would have saved us some time."

"I think you're wrong, detective. Ms. Remington is not a violent person."

"The victims always think that."

He was laughing when he hung up.

"I could have told you her birthday," Sharon said. "But I wouldn't have. You men have to learn the hard way."

"Did your husband learn the hard way?"

"It involved a vase; maybe I'll tell you about it sometime."

She smiled. I had visions of a vase coursing through the air. I also had visions of Remington, keeping her elbow up and following through on the pitch. I tried not to dwell on that.

It was only 9 A.M. Since I now had a respectable job and position on the paper, I was keeping respectable office hours. No one else on my staff was. Robert had a council meeting that night, so I wouldn't see him before noon; and Sherri was off at some school function. I had opened the mail (it took me about half an hour every day) and was now ready to work. Only I didn't have any work to do yet. What good is an editor when there's nothing around to edit?

I saw — and smelled — the resumé that Margaret had left me. It smelled just like her. I think I once dated a girl who wore that perfume.

The resumé was a standard format, listing jobs and duties. At the bottom were the phone numbers of some of the places she'd worked. She'd mainly been in sales. I reached for the phone and dialed the first number. It turned out to be a car dealership in Austin.

"Is Mr. Epps there?" I asked, looking at the name of her immediate supervisor.

"One moment," a woman's voice said.

"Epps," a man said a moment later.

"My name is Emerson Dunn," I said. "I'm checking some references on a Margaret Sullivan, who says she used to work for you. Do you recall her?"

"Friend, that was years ago," he said after a pause. "I don't remember much. I was the sales manager over the used cars then. She wasn't bad, I don't guess, but she wasn't here long. Can't help you much, other than to tell you she didn't run off with one of our cars or the boss's son or anything like that."

I looked at the date listed on her resumé; I guess I hadn't looked closely at it before. She'd left that job more than five years ago.

"Thank you, sir," I said. "I appreciate the help."

I hung up and looked at the dates on the other jobs. According to her resumé, she hadn't worked for about four years. She certainly didn't look like someone who hadn't eaten for that length of time. Perhaps she was married and was raising kids at home; but her resumé listed her marital status as "single" and mentioned no children.

And she hadn't struck me as the homemaker type. June Cleaver never looked like that.

Several calls later I knew very little more about her. Her last job was with a jewelry store, selling diamonds and watches. She also designed a few pieces and even made some of her own jewelry, the resumé said.

All right, maybe she'd been in business for herself for the past four years, making and selling jewelry.

I didn't believe that for a second. She didn't seem the entrepreneur type.

I gave up for the moment and started to write an editorial supporting the city's efforts to beef up city code enforcement (that kind of thing can make the city look better, and this city needed all the help it could get). It was tough; I was on the verge of boring myself to death. (Going nose-down on our keyboards is how we newspaper people secretly fear we'll leave this world.)

At about 1:00 Robert walked in, looking hot. He was wearing slacks and a sport coat. Robert was fresh out of college and had somehow gotten it into his head that this was a real job, the kind where you dress up and all. Boy, did he have a lot to learn.

"Let's get some lunch," I said to him before he could sit down. "I'll buy."

He smiled.

"But you can't take your coat," I said. "This is July."

He nodded, as if I were his boss or something, and hung his sport coat on the coatrack behind Sharon's desk. Although it was the middle of the day, the newsroom was still empty. On the other side, where the ad reps sit, the desks were empty too. The ad reps were out selling ads and making us money. Even Louise hadn't been in yet; but since she would stay late that night and help me lay out the paper, I couldn't complain.

The afternoon was humid and a little too hot, even for this time of year. We got into my car and drove up Commerce Street to Zarape, the small restaurant owned by Walter and Gunther Schmidt. As I had hoped, the parking lot was clearing. I wasn't in the mood to deal with people. Robert followed me into the small gas station-turned-restaurant. I'd been there often enough to be a part-owner in the place, but no one bothered to offer me stock options.

"Herr Dunn," came a voice from behind the counter. "Guten abend. Und Herr Matthews."

"Ja, guten abend," I said as we found a booth. "Dos schnitzel, por favor."

"You mix your languages again," Walter said as he emerged wearing a flour-coated apron. "Shall I bring the usual?"

"Please."

Walter bowed and started to turn on his heel when he paused. "And everything is in order for Thursday night?"

Robert looked blank. I'm sure I looked blank for a moment too, until I realized what he was talking about.

Dinner for two at 8 P.M., when the restaurant closed. It was to be a private candlelight dinner complete with a birthday cake for Remington. I vaguely recalled discussing such a scenario with the guys a month or so ago. They'd remembered.

"No, everything is *not* in order, Herr Schmidt," I said. "I almost forgot. She had to remind me."

Walter, a handsome, thirty-five-year-old German chef (he'd been to *school*, as he often reminded us), grinned and pulled up a chair from a nearby table. He turned it around and sat facing us.

"Not to worry," he said. "Dinner and the apfel cake will be ready. Have you bought her a present yet? Ah, I can see from your expression that you have not. So young. You are lucky to have me here. I know the thinking of a woman. I will help you."

Above Walter's shoulder I saw his brother approaching, dishrag in hand.

"He knows the thinking of a woman? Ask him when he last had a date," Gunther said. "If he knows the thinking of a woman, why does he live with me?"

I smiled at Robert as the German expletives started flying. We kept low to avoid the flak and just watched. The argument — one which had been going on at least since I'd known the boys

— seemed to center on two points. The first was, of course, that Walter knew everything and that Gunther knew nothing. The second point, the view favored more by Gunther himself, was that Walter only *thought* he knew everything, but in fact recently had to call me up to find out how to spell the word *sausage* for the new menu. Gunther also maintained that Walter's strudel was vastly inferior to his own. Walter countered that Gunther was always a bad brother and was most probably adopted. The few lunchtime customers who remained watched in bewilderment.

About five minutes later the discussion ended with the pronouncement by Gunther that Walter's mediocre schnitzel was burning, which would probably help the taste and certainly the texture of the dish. Walter stormed off to the kitchen, still flinging curses.

I never did get that help he offered.

Gunther sat down in the chair recently occupied by his brother.

"So, Emerson, you will buy her a ring?" Gunther asked.

I felt my throat tighten. I felt my palms start to sweat. I also felt it was time to leave the country.

I swallowed and took a deep breath. "Let's not rush things, Gunth. I was thinking more along the lines of a nice pen and pencil set. Or maybe a blender. I don't know what they use them for, but women seem to like blenders."

"Oh no, that will never do," came a voice from behind me.

I looked over my shoulder at a woman I'd never seen before.

"You show up with that, she'll never speak to you again," she added.

I turned more to face her. She looked about fifty-five, with big hair (reddish, a shade probably not found in nature), bright red nails, and crinkles around her mouth and eyes from a lifetime of smiling too much. Probably a realtor. Or maybe she sold cosmetics.

"You know Remington?"

Roy Maynard

"I don't have to." The woman smiled. "I know a woman's thinking."

She grinned, and I couldn't help but do the same.

"So what do you suggest?" I asked.

"It has to be jewelry. Something nice that she can show off. It doesn't have to be a ring. A necklace perhaps. With matching earrings. What are her colors?"

I wasn't sure how to respond.

"Her colors," the woman said impatiently. "You men . . . All right, what color are most of her dresses?"

"Uh, pastel. She likes pastels. See, I knew that."

"Then she's probably a spring."

I was about ready to bail out of this conversation when the woman took out a notepad and scribbled something down. She stood and brought the scrap of paper to me.

"Stick with any one of these stones," she said. "They're cheaper than diamonds — not as committal but still elegant."

I looked at the list. The only stone I recognized was sapphire, which was my ex-fiancée Julie's favorite. I thought back to a necklace I'd once given to her a few years ago. When I remembered the look on Julie's face, I decided that this slightly pushy, overly perfumed dame might be right.

"OK," I said, "you've convinced me. I'll hit the mall later this afternoon."

She shook her head and took the slip of paper from my hand. She scribbled another list on it.

"Call these places first. Good prices, good people to deal with. They'll rook you in the malls."

She took a twenty dollar bill from her purse and left it on the table where she'd been sitting, then started to leave.

"Who are you?" I asked.

"Maybe your guardian angel, " she said. "Or hers. A boy once gave me a brand-new pop-up bread toaster for my birthday. That was years ago, in college. I'm sure I needed one, but it was the

28

most unromantic gift I'd ever received. I never spoke to him again."

She paused and smiled again.

"And it's too bad I didn't. He's now making a fortune as a tax attorney."

She left in a cloud of Chanel No. 5.

"What was that all about?" Robert asked.

"I don't know, but I'm not completely ready to disregard the part about her being my guardian angel. I somehow always knew that mine would have big hair and a manicure."

I stuffed the scrap of paper into my shirt pocket as Walter came back with four cups of coffee. Only one table was left of the lunchtime crowd, and they looked about finished. After politely checking to see if they needed anything, Walter sat down beside me in the booth.

"You will want music, no?" he asked.

"I hadn't thought about it."

"You will have music."

"Nothing involving tubas, thank you," I said. "I know how you Germans are with that oompah stuff."

Walter bowed with a serious look on his face. "I will find something romantic."

"And no Wagner either," I said. "I do like Beethoven, though. Think you can handle it?"

He harumphed and sipped his coffee.

"Walter, what was Mrs. Tate's check?" Gunther asked as he rose to get the twenty dollar bill off the table where my angel had sat.

Walter reached into an apron pocket and pulled out an order pad.

"It was $3.75," he said. "She had just a salad."

"She does this again," he said, handing the twenty dollars to his brother. Walter sighed, and Gunther turned to me.

"She is a new customer," Gunther said. "But she is already a regular, and she never takes her change."

"Perhaps she is our angel too, no?" Walter said.

"Maybe," I said.

Over coffee, we talked about Life in General. Robert said he was starting to get comfortable in the small-town atmosphere. It wouldn't last, I could have told him. Soon he'd look for bigger and better things. He certainly had the talent for it.

I'd worked for a big paper before, and to be honest, I liked this pace better. But I knew the *Times* was a stepping-stone for Robert, and that was fine. I'd rather have a kid with ambition on my staff for only a year or so than to have an unmotivated reporter hanging on for ten or twelve. Robert still felt a little restless; I liked that in a reporter. In fact, I had to admit I liked Robert.

Walter and Gunther went on for a bit about the plans for Thursday night. I mentally went through my financial portfolio and decided I had enough cash on hand to actually buy a present, pay for the birthday meal, and still pay my electric bill. It was a new feeling, this financial solvency. I was beginning to get comfortable myself.

Comfortable. That's always a dangerous place to be.

3

A few hours later I walked into a hole-in-the-wall jewelry shop at the north end of town. It was at the top of the list the woman with the big hair and fingernails had given me. I'd seen this place, but they didn't advertise with us and I'd never had occasion to buy any jewelry, so I had never been inside. But I did know the man at the counter.

Mordechai was peering through one of those swing-arm jeweler's magnifiers at a bracelet he seemed to be fixing with his thick, meaty fingers. This jewelry store must have been the business he'd told me he bought.

"Good afternoon," he said with a smile, as if he were remembering how much we'd laughed the night before. "What may I do for you, Emerson? Is this a social call or business? You know, I would like to buy ads."

"I need some jewelry," I said. "I don't sell the ads, but I can send someone by. Right now, though, I need to make a purchase."

He lifted his eyes and looked at the lighted display cases lining the shop. He was wearing the same hat and prayer shawl, but his suit coat was off and his sleeves were rolled up.

"Jewelry we have," he said, nodding. He turned his attention back to the bracelet.

I browsed through the shop until I got to a case full of sapphire jewelry; several nice necklaces stood out. At least I think they were nice. What did I know about jewelry?

"How much is this one?" I asked, pointing.

Mordechai looked over. He lifted his nose and peered down it, as if that would give him a better perspective on matters.

"That depends," he said.

"On what?"

"What time is it?"

I looked at my watch. "4:15 P.M."

"Ah!" he said, slamming a meaty fist down on the counter for effect. "That is the exact time of the day when I am the most charitable. You knew this, no? You plan this? OK, so what can I do? I'll make you a good deal."

I grinned. This character wanted to bargain. I was ready. I was a man of the world.

He stood and marched around the counter to the back of the display case. He opened it and retrieved the necklace. It had a price marked on the bottom that I caught a glimpse of: $295, with no decimal points anywhere in sight. I started having doubts. I started thinking that maybe I could get a plane ticket out of the country for that much money.

"This, this is a very valuable piece," he said. "It is worth much. But for you, you who are family, you who are almost a brother to my nephew, I give you a deal."

I was dreading the next part.

"$100," he said. "And not a penny less. No sir."

It took a moment for me to remember how to work my mouth.

"But, Mordechai . . ."

"You're ungrateful and a hard man," he said. "But OK — just $75. Nothing less or you take food from the mouths of my children."

"You don't have any children."

"You make light of a man's misery? You joke that he has no family, that his only love is his business, and then you try to take even that from him by forcing his prices down? I should have listened to my grandmother, who was very wise, when she told me, 'Mordechai, you cannot be a businessman, your heart is too soft. You should be a doctor.' But I didn't listen. And now I pay for that mistake. All right, $50. But you will not sleep tonight."

"Mordechai, I want to pay the *real* price," I said. "Look, on the bottom it says $295. I'll pay that."

"You will not pay that!" he thundered, his gestures getting more and more emphatic. "That is not a price! That is not *my* price. That is fiction!"

He sighed, took a handkerchief from his pocket, and wiped his forehead. He leaned down onto the counter and motioned for me to come closer.

"Emerson, I tell you true," he whispered in a store with no one in it but us. "You helped me buy this place. The former owner? You and my nephew, you helped put him in jail. The bank, it foreclosed. I got a good deal on the building, the inventory, everything. Now I give you a good deal. And I want to see this necklace on the neck of — what was her name? Remington? — at dinner on Sabbath. Make an old man happy."

"When I see an old man, I'll do that," I whispered back. "But I'm not going to take this necklace for a penny less than $250."

He went off again. "My heart, it cannot take this strain. Where is your mother? I want to call her and tell her she has a son who does not respect the old. It is $150, and I never want to see your face again — until Friday."

"No. I will pay $200, and you will not call my mother, because if you do, I will tell your sister that you tried to give me a bad deal. And she still has that knife."

The poor man went white. The deal was done.

He grumbled in Hebrew the whole time he was wrapping my purchase. He grumbled when he took my money and shooed me out the door like a small child who was getting in the way of business.

It wasn't until I got back to the office and took it out to show

Sharon that I realized he'd put a pair of matching earrings into the box as well.

Tuesday night was when we put together the Thursday edition of our twice-a-week paper. Robert came in with his city council story at about 9 P.M., and Louise and I had the paper put together and proofed by 11 P.M.

I liked Louise. After my last publisher had been sacked, Louise came in from one of the weekly papers in our chain with some new ideas. She was a very professional woman; she was about forty, unmarried, and very good at what she did. She let me upgrade the darkroom so we wouldn't asphyxiate poor David with the bad ventilation, and she let me hire two good reporters at decent salaries. She wasn't afraid to work either. My biggest weakness was page design; I could get it done, but she was much more creative about it. She could make a front page jump right out of the newsstand at you.

"Get out of here," she said politely as we put the finishing touches on the Thursday edition. "Go home, and don't come in early tomorrow. You've been here fifteen hours today."

"Well, if you insist," I said. "I could use some extra sleep."

I could have, too, but I never got it. I should have known. My plans were changed about thirty seconds later when we sensed the explosion.

It was the kind of explosion that you don't hear — you *feel* it. In our office we felt a thud, and we knew something somewhere was very, very wrong. The police scanner immediately went crazy. The only information the dispatcher had was an approximate location: Holiday Inn, a few blocks up from the newspaper office on Commerce Street. Louise was beeping David as I ran for my car with a notebook in hand. On a good day we can beat the Volunteer Fire Department.

A few squad cars were ahead of me as I ripped up Commerce Street, fracturing one or two traffic laws in the process. I could see flames coming from what used to be an automobile in the Holiday Inn parking lot.

We all parked, and I just tried to stay out of the way until the cops felt like they had the crime scene under control.

And it was most definitely a crime scene. I've seen cars catch on fire from something as simple as a leak in a gasoline line. But cars burn — they don't blow up in real life like they do on TV shows. Not when they're sitting squarely in a parking space, motionless, as this one had been. This one hadn't burned, it had blown up. The burning was a minor aftereffect.

I had a sudden sinking feeling. I saw a cop I knew creeping up as close as he could to the driver's side; he was looking for a body. I took a breath when I saw him shake his head to his patrol sergeant.

I started walking toward the patrol sergeant when I felt my foot kicking something. I looked down at a hubcap. I looked up at the car, still fifty feet away. That was a major explosion, no doubt.

"Dunn, don't ask me any questions because I don't have any answers," said Sergeant Joel Harris. "Singer will be here in a few minutes, and maybe he'll tell you something. All I know is that someone's pretty Mustang is melting onto the parking lot."

I looked closer; it did appear to be a Mustang.

Singer and David arrived at about the same time. David immediately started snapping photos, making up for the darkness with a flash and strategic use of the light coming from the streetlamp over that part of the parking lot.

Bill Singer, a stocky, somewhat rough-around-the-edges cop I'd known since I'd first gotten to town, wasn't pleased. He usually wasn't pleased to be called out at night. He usually *was* pleased to see me, but he just had trouble showing it. At least that's what I told myself.

"Dunn, did you cause this?" he asked.

For him, that was the usual assumption.

"Not this time," I said. "I just got here myself. And I have an alibi."

He grunted and walked over to the car. The Volunteer Fire

Department had about put the flames out. Singer gave the car a lengthy once-over and then a twice-over.

He marched back up to me to release his statement.

"At approximately 11:10 P.M. a late-model Ford exploded in the parking lot of the Holiday Inn."

"That's it? I knew that before you got here."

"You're just never satisfied, are you, Dunn?"

"Do you suspect arson?"

"Arson? No, I don't expect arson. I expect an inexpertly wired car bomb."

David was back; he raised his eyebrows at the mention of car bombs. He'd had some experience with those in the streets of Beirut.

"What makes you think it was a car bomb?" I asked.

"All four tires were blown out, suggesting an explosion centered around the undercarriage of the automobile."

"And also because the transmission is now in the front seat," David added with a grin.

"I cannot confirm nor deny that," Singer said with a grin of his own. "We don't know for sure if that transmission is from this car or not."

In other words, someone taped a pipe bomb under the car and it went off a little too soon. It didn't take the driver with it, but that Mustang was officially out to pasture.

A patrol officer walked up to Singer and looked nervously at us.

"Talk," Singer said. "These guys are harmless. They won't print anything they're not supposed to, because they know what kind of food we serve at the jail."

The officer, a Hispanic woman, said, "We've run the plates. The car is registered to one Margaret Sullivan, address in Corpus Christi."

"Then go ask the bellboy or the night desk person where we may find Ms. Sullivan," Singer said with strained patience. "Why do I have to do everyone's thinking for them?"

What a grouch. I figured it was the wretched coffee they served at the police station. But I had more important things to worry about, such as one Margaret Sullivan.

David looked at me; I nodded. He recognized the name, even though I'd only mentioned it to him once. He was a sharp guy. Margaret Sullivan, our Mystery Job Hunter. I had meant to call her back that day, to tell her I hadn't found anything and I'd checked everywhere a regular personnel manager would.

I'd played fair, just like Sally had asked. But someone else wasn't. I was just glad she wasn't in the car.

As if by some prearranged plan, David kept Singer busy by asking permission to get up close and get some shots. He knew Singer wouldn't grant it, but since Singer was mostly a by-the-book cop, he'd have to come up with a reason before saying no.

Meanwhile, I slinked over to Room 111, the address Margaret had given me. I knocked. Nothing. I tried the door. Locked.

I wandered back to Singer and David as two patrol officers started marching toward Room 111. The desk person must have told them where Margaret Sullivan was staying.

"Well, Dave, I say we get this back to the office and onto page 1 before Louise sends it to press without us," I said. "Let's go."

David looked at me funny. He knew that our courier Jimmy wouldn't take the pages to be printed until about 2 A.M. The printing press was on a tight schedule, and it wouldn't do any good to get our paper there early. David knew we had some time, but being the trusting soul that he is, he followed me to our cars.

"I don't understand any of this, but we'd better find Margaret Sullivan and soon," I said as we reached my Ford and his Toyota.

"I think we just did," he said.

Sitting in the passenger seat of my car was a drop-dead gorgeous blonde. I thought I heard that saxophone again.

don't need anything in that room," she said. "I don't want to go back."

I was driving down Commerce Street trying to keep my attention on the road. David was ahead of me; he had film he needed to process. I had a blonde I needed to talk into going to the police. They'd be looking for her.

"You've got to make a report," I said. "You can't be afraid of these cops; Sally Nix is one of them."

The blonde nodded.

"It's not the cops I'm worried about," she said. "It's going back there. If someone could find my car there, they could find me. Maybe he's there right now, watching."

"Who's 'he'?"

"Someone I want to forget about."

That's all I could get out of her. She just sat there, dressed in the same ivory blouse with a gray skirt; her purse was in between us. We were getting close to the office; I knew I had to get her to the cops.

"Look, how about if I take you to the police station? Surely this bad guy won't be there. Bad guys don't like police stations, as a rule."

She thought about it, then nodded.

"Fine. One condition. You don't leave me there."

"OK. I can call in my story from the station, or just write it up later tonight," I said. "But what about afterwards? Where will you stay?"

"You can't leave me."

"OK, I won't leave you until you say it's OK. Sally said you could trust me. You can, I guess."

I had this vision of a wrathful Remington . . . I somehow didn't think she'd understand me putting up a mysterious blonde on my couch.

And then I smiled. No, I wouldn't have to put up the blonde, because Remington would do it. She'd do it gladly once I explained to her that the alternative was keeping said floozy at my place.

We drove to the police station and parked in the "chief" spot. He wouldn't be up at this hour; he was smarter than that. That's how he got to be chief. We went inside, and I asked the dispatcher to call Singer and tell him I'd found the car's owner. Then we went back and waited in his office.

He walked in about five minutes later.

"Dunn, don't get mixed up in police matters again," he said. "And where did you find Ms. Sullivan, if that's who this is?"

"It is," Margaret said. "And he found me in the front seat of his car."

Singer raised his eyebrows.

"Don't get ideas, Bill," I said. "Margaret Sullivan is a friend of —"

"That's not important," she said, cutting me off. "I just want to make a statement and leave."

"It might be more serious than that," Singer said, walking around his small office and sitting behind his desk. "Do you think someone is trying to kill you?"

Margaret turned her head. They do that sometimes in the old movies. I think it meant she didn't want to answer the question.

"Who?" Singer said gently.

"No one," Margaret said, turning back to face him. "Let's just get this over with. I was in the lounge of the hotel when I heard a noise, and I saw my car on fire. That's all I know."

Singer sighed. He had much more patience than he usually let on, but I think he was starting to realize that Margaret Sullivan had no intention of cooperating.

"Are you in trouble?" he asked.

"No."

"You don't want any police protection?"

"No."

"Then get her out of here, Dunn, and keep her at an address where we can find her."

He stared at her for a moment.

"Miss, we can't help you if you won't let us. If there was anything I could charge you with and keep you here in jail, I'd do it just to keep you safe. Dunn, get rid of her."

I nodded and stood. She stood up, grabbed her purse, and stormed past me.

"Bill, what are we going to do?"

"I'll run her driver's license number, and you and that one-man Israeli demolition team of yours keep her safe. A car bomb means she made someone mad. We'll try to find out who."

I started to leave.

"Dunn, I need to know one thing — is Nix involved in this? That would tell me a lot."

I hesitated; Margaret obviously didn't want Sally Nix brought into this. But that hesitation was enough for Singer.

"Dunn, do you know who Nix is working with?"

"No."

"The vice section of an organized crime task force in Nueces County. The same county that Mustang was registered in. I emphasize the *was*."

"That still doesn't tell us anything."

"No, but Sally might."

I nodded. "You're on the right track."

I left the office as Singer was picking up his telephone.

"Well, Detective Sergeant Singer didn't give me time to call in my story," I said to Margaret as I got into my car. She was already sitting on the passenger's side. "We'll have to swing by the office so I can punch it out. Is that OK with you?"

"Sure."

When we got to the newspaper office, I just had time to type up a quick eight-inch story and slap it down in place of a school board piece that could wait. We replaced the front-page art with a shot of some firefighters extinguishing the burning car; David had done some good work. Jimmy was grumbling about the time as I handed him the box full of pages.

In the story I went light on the facts about the owner of the car. The public has a right to know a lot of things, but until I knew who this girl was, I wasn't going to give a mad bomber any more leads. Margaret sat at my desk, reading copies of old newspapers.

I sent David home as soon as his photos were done. I knew I might need him early the next morning.

When Jimmy left, just before 2 A.M., I grabbed the phone in the composing room (out of earshot of Margaret).

"Remington, are you awake?"

"No. What do you want?"

"Remember the floozy? She needs to bunk with you — maybe for a few nights."

There was silence at the other end of the line.

"Or I could let her stay at my place," I added.

"Bring her by," Remington said. "I'll be up."

The security guard at the gate of the apartment complex waved me on by as we pulled up to where Remington lived (she'd moved into a nicer complex after she'd gotten on with the Houston paper — or more precisely, she had me and David move her when she'd gotten on with the Houston paper).

Remington didn't look happy when she answered the door a few minutes later. Margaret looked even less so.

"A. C. Remington, this is Margaret Sullivan," I said as I ushered the blonde into my girlfriend's apartment. "Remington is a reporter for a Houston paper. She's pretty good. And, Remington, I have no idea who Margaret is or what she does or why she's here."

Margaret didn't seem phased by my intended abruptness. She wasn't upset in the least that I didn't have that information, and she didn't seem as if she particularly wanted to divulge it to me.

Margaret looked around the apartment for a moment, as if casing the place. She checked the locks on the doors to see if they were secure; she then set her purse down on Remington's coffee table and herself down on Remington's couch.

And promptly started crying.

Remington kicked into high gear. The blonde was no longer a floozy, but now someone in distress. I'd noticed that about Remington. Regular church attendance was having an effect. As a reporter, she knew full well the enormity and sheer number of the needs out there. As a Christian, she was starting to realize that she could do something about some of them, and that sometimes that was enough.

Remington was on the couch comforting Margaret; I was simply in the way.

"Remington, her car was blown up tonight, and we don't know why," I said. "If she knows, she's not telling. I don't know if she's in danger. Do you two want me to stay?"

Margaret looked at Remington, and somehow some kind of communication passed between them. Remington looked back up at me.

"No, we'll be fine," Remington said. "But what about tomorrow? I've got to go to work."

"I'll think of something. Drop her off at my place on your way out of town."

"See you."

I left but didn't go home. I dropped by the police station and wasn't surprised to see Detective Sergeant Bill Singer's car still there.

"Do you know anything yet?" I asked as I walked into his office.

He looked up at me.

"A little. I called Sally at her apartment down in Corpus. Get us both some coffee, swear to me that we're off the record, and I'll tell you the whole story."

I got up and got the coffee. As I sat down, Singer handed me an 8 x 10 glossy; it was a professional shot of Margaret. He said he found it in her hotel room.

"Name, Margaret Sullivan. No warrants. No criminal history. A few bounced checks, nothing more. Until last week she was an exotic dancer."

"How exotic?"

"She was a convertible, my friend," Singer said. "Sally met her at a topless club the task force is investigating. Somehow Margaret duped Sally into believing that she really wanted to get out of the business. So Sally helped her, as best as she could. Sally helped Margaret doctor her resumé and pick out some socially acceptable clothes. She coached Margaret on how to interview for jobs and then, as a final test, sent her to you. Sally figured that if you couldn't find out that Margaret Sullivan — who danced under the name Meagan — was a topless dancer, no one else could either."

"So the note from Sally was sincere."

"But apparently Margaret wasn't. The night Margaret left, so did about $50,000 in cash. Margaret got away with every cookie in the jar, and the owner of the club is not a happy man."

"This doesn't add up, Bill."

"How so?"

"First of all, if you've got an embezzlement charge against Margaret, why haven't you asked me where she is? And second, if Margaret ran away with the money, why did she run straight to me, where Sally would know where to find her?"

"The owner has not filed any charges, so officially I don't care where you've stashed the blonde. And I don't know why she's here. What I do know is that someone's setting off bombs in my city, and my guess is the owner wants to take care of business himself."

"What's Sally's exposure in all of this? When she trusted Margaret, was her cover blown?"

"Wide open. Margaret knows she's a cop, and we don't know who else knows. So Nueces County has pulled Nix off the investigation, and we're sending her on a little vacation for a couple of weeks, to a safe place. A distant safe place."

I nodded.

"What now?" I asked.

"I don't know. With no charges, I can't keep her locked up. Maybe you can keep her safe until we figure out what's going on. After the owner of this nightclub is taken in, maybe she'll be safe."

"What are they after him for? Prostitution?"

"Come on, Dunn, there's no money in that anymore. Cocaine — that's where the money is. By the way, in addition to the fifty grand that was taken, rumor has it that close to a kilo was lifted. Sally hasn't confirmed that yet. But you might check your new girlfriend's purse."

"My new girlfriend?"

"She's sure taken a liking to you, buddy," he said with a grin. "Let's hope you live through it."

I slept soundly that night until about 11 A.M. — when I woke up and realized that a strange woman was asleep on my couch. I snuck through the living room, wondering whether to peek in her purse or not, just to check on that kilo of cocaine. But I didn't. I was almost out of the room and into the kitchen when I heard the ruffle of a blanket.

I also heard the unmistakable sound of a bullet being chambered into an automatic pistol. That got my attention.

"Oh, it's you," Margaret said as I slowly turned around. I saw her lower a chrome pistol that had been pointed at my head.

"Kinda jumpy this morning, aren't you?"

"I'm sorry."

"No need to apologize. Just try not to let a perfectly nice morning be upset with a nasty death, namely mine. Tell you what, I'm going to clean up, then I'll fix you some breakfast."

I emerged from the shower a few minutes later, got dressed, and went back into the living room.

"I think we need to talk," I said.

She was dressed in jeans and a T-shirt I recognized as Remington's. She looked a little better than someone who had been through a night like last night should be allowed to look. I tried to ignore that.

"Talking isn't one of my favorite pastimes," she said. "Let's not. Let's just eat."

"Sorry, but I've got a dangerous woman with a gun in my living room, so I think I'm entitled to some answers. Let me start: did you take the money?"

"What money?"

"Right. Well, then, where is the kilo of cocaine?"

"I don't know what you're talking about."

"Then why did you come here?"

"Sally said I could trust you."

"Could Sally trust you?" I asked. "Or did you blow her cover and put her in danger?"

"I wouldn't do that; she's my friend. My only friend. Except for you."

"What makes you think I'm your friend?"

"You took me to your girlfriend's house. Most men would have taken me straight to their own beds — or at least tried to. You didn't."

On that note, I went into the kitchen to fix some coffee. I needed it. As it started dripping through the filter and down into the decanter, I went back into the living room. Margaret was putting on some sneakers I also recognized as Remington's.

"How can I be your friend if you're not going to be honest with me?"

She sighed. "You want honest?"

"Yeah, it goes well with coffee."

"I had to get out. Sally helped me. I came to see you. My car was blown up. That's all I know."

"What's the name of the club you worked at?"

"Is that important?"

"No. But what's the name of the owner?"

"Garrett Maxwell. We called him Max. He's not a nice man. He seems like a nice man at first, but then . . ."

"Now we're getting somewhere."

I fixed her some coffee; she drank it black, like I do. She was finishing her second cup when the phone rang.

"Hello?" I answered.

"Emerson, can you come to my store? This is Mordechai. I must talk to you."

"Sure. When?"

"Now. And, Emerson, bring the girl."

I stopped cold. No one knew I had her with me.

"Mordechai, what girl are you speaking of?"

"David said her name was Margaret, and he told me about her. Someone came into my store this morning . . . You must come . . . Now. Bring her."

His voice registered a commanding tone I hadn't heard before. Even when he was trying to sell me the jewelry at a ridiculous price, he hadn't been so forceful.

But he was David's uncle. If I couldn't trust him, who could I trust?

"I'll be there soon."

I hung up and grabbed my keys. I didn't bother to dry my hair, which was still damp.

"Come on," I said. "We're going to see a friend. At least, I hope he's a friend."

Margaret looked a little nervous, but she didn't want to be left alone.

"And we're leaving this here unless you have a permit for it,"

I said, taking the gun from the couch and putting it on top of my bookshelf. Margaret looked even more nervous.

"Where did you get it, by the way?" I asked.

"Let's say it was the only souvenir I kept from a former life."

She said nothing more as we walked out the door.

"Stay low in the car," I said. "If your friend with the dynamite is out and about today, I wouldn't want him getting any ideas about blowing up this car. No siree bob. This is one valuable piece of machinery."

I almost got a smile out of her.

5

We drove north to Mordechai's hole-in-the-wall jewelry store. A single car was parked outside; it had the new-car paper license plates on it. We walked in, and only Mordechai was in the store.

"Ah, as I feared. It is her," he said.

"It is who?" I asked, looking around for signs of anything amiss. But when I looked into Mordechai's eyes again, I realized that nothing would be. His were the eyes of a protector.

"A boy, about your age, Emerson, came into my shop today," Mordechai said. "He brought me a photo. It was her. He asked me if she had come in, perhaps for a job or perhaps to sell me some jewelry. He said the jewelry would be handmade, good work. Then he took a ring off his finger and showed it to me; he told me she made it for him. I said it is nice, it is a very fine piece. I look through my magnifier, I look at it closely. I asked him, 'Why do you want to find her?' He said, 'Because I love her.' I said, 'That is good, it is good to love someone.'"

I looked at Margaret. Her back had stiffened up.

"Go on," I said.

Mordechai looked down his nose at her, sizing her up.

"Not now," he said. "More later. For now, I want you to leave her here. Miss, what shall I call you?"

"Maggie," she said.

I smiled. There was something not only protective but also paternal about this old Jew. Margaret had picked up on it.

"Then, Maggie, I can't have you everywhere in my way," he said. "There are some watches in the back room, they need fixing. Most need batteries. You know how to fix these, yes?"

"Yes."

"Then go. And we'll order out for pizza. They'll bring it to me because they know how important I am. They'll say, 'Yes, sir, we'll bring it to you in thirty minutes' because they know I am not a patient man. They fear to bring it to me late."

"Mordechai, they bring it to everyone in less than thirty minutes," I said.

He looked down his nose at me.

"But do they say, 'Yes, sir' to everyone?"

I smiled. Margaret was already heading for the back room. I walked over to Mordechai.

"My friend, here is a name and an address," he said when she was out of sight. "This is the young man who is looking for this girl. He tells me that if I see her, to please contact him. Find out who he is. But don't trust him. And take David with you."

"Why?"

"Do you need to know? Can you not simply do as I ask?"

"I don't trust easily these days," I said. "I'm not even sure I should be trusting you."

He didn't respond to that. I looked into his kind face.

"Mordechai, exactly what did you do in the army?"

"Many things. I'm a colonel. I can take care of Maggie. And I have a friend, a lady friend, who will help. But, Emerson, you have work to do. Why do you stand around here asking about my love life?"

"You mentioned your lady friend, not me."

"Then go away. I have work."

I left, feeling reasonably good about leaving Margaret in capable hands. I drove to the office and found David sitting at my desk.

"Did you go see Uncle Mordechai?"

"Yes."

"Then let's go."

"Now? David, we have work to do."

"Take off, Dunn," Louise said, coming out of her office. "David says you boys need some time off. I don't know if I believe that, but you do have some comp time coming to you. I'll see you Thursday."

David grinned.

I grabbed the phone and called Remington at her Pasadena office. I told her about the missing money and cocaine.

"Don't be too quick to judge the girl," Remington said. "I don't think she took anything like that. I spent about two hours talking with her last night. I believe her."

"Let's hope you're right. See you at church tonight."

I hung up, and David followed me toward the door.

Sharon was at her desk, taking a classified ad over the phone. I scribbled out a note to her that said I'd be in touch and dropped it on her desk as David and I walked out the door toward his car. David, a 6'2" guy with short, black hair, a muscular build, and a certain fondness for wearing his photographer's vest everywhere we went, was excited.

"What do you mean, we need time off?" I asked as we reached his car.

"Didn't Uncle Mordechai give you an address?"

"Yes." I took it out and looked at it. But it wasn't an address at all, really; it was the number of a boat slip in the Galveston Yacht Basin. It seems our mystery man had sailed here.

The drive down State Highway 6 was quick. David really didn't know much at all about our little outing. Apparently Mordechai had simply called him and told him to accompany me to see this guy, and David obeyed without question. I guess when your uncle is a colonel, you do that sort of thing.

I told David everything Singer had told me — all about Sally Nix's investigation, the nightclub where she met Margaret, and what Margaret had been doing. David nodded a lot, asked a few questions, but didn't seem bothered by any of it. I guess when you've lived through a holiday in Beirut, very little bothers you.

I looked at my watch; it was nearly 2 P.M.

We crossed over the causeway onto the island and drove down Port Industrial Boulevard to the Yacht Basin. I flashed a press card at the kid in the guardhouse, and he waved us on. We drove into the parking lot and stopped. David parked his car and started gathering his gear.

"Now wait, we don't have a plan," I said. "What are we going to do?"

"That's easy," he said. "Do what you do best: ask questions. Who doesn't like to talk about themselves?"

With the recent exception of Margaret Sullivan, David was right. We wandered toward the boat slip Mordechai had told us about. As we neared it, I could see a mid-1970s O'Day sailboat, twenty-eight feet long with an autopilot and some navigational equipment and antennas. A young, good-looking man was aboard, washing down the deck with a hose hooked up to a faucet on the dock.

"Been offshore?" I asked. The autopilot meant the sailboat wasn't just for day trips.

"Yeah," the guy said. "I just sailed up from Corpus. My first blue-water trip alone."

"Nice boat," I said.

"Thanks. What's with the cameras?"

He pointed at David's bag, obviously suspicious of our presence.

"We're from the local paper," I said. "We come down here every once in a while to see what or who has blown in. We get some good stories sometimes. Anyone who's been offshore has some good stories. You got one?"

The guy grinned; "Yeah, I got one. But you can't print it. Wanna come aboard?"

We walked across a gangplank onto his small boat. At twenty-eight feet, it was definitely lot bigger than mine (a mere sixteen-footer), but out in the ocean or the Gulf, it still would seem pretty small.

"Have a seat," he said as we sat in the cockpit. He went below and quickly emerged with three cans of Coke.

"Hope this will do," he said. "It's all I've got."

We thanked him and leaned back as he started talking.

"My name is Brian Putnam. I'm from Corpus. I was working in a bar there, as kind of a gopher for the owner. Well, I met this girl — she worked at the bar. We started going out, and boy, I fell hard. I mean, I really loved this girl. We had a plan, see; we'd buy this boat and sail away. We'd go to Bermuda, the Bahamas, maybe even Jamaica. It was a good plan. I sold my truck, but I was still about $5,000 short to buy this boat. So she lends it to me. She says it's kind of her boat too. Maybe her home someday. So we take lessons together, we learn to sail it, and we outfit it to live aboard. We set a date; we were going to leave on July 4 — Independence Day. Ironic, huh? But that was a few weeks ago. A lot can change."

Brian took a sip of his Coke, squinted at the sun, and continued. "So the week before we were supposed to leave, she starts getting weird, you know? I mean, we'd start stowing our gear, and she'd keep forgetting to bring her stuff. We'd meet at the boat, she'd be empty-handed. So we'd stow my stuff, and I left room for her things. I figured we'd just pack it all in at the last minute. Well, on July 3 she disappears. *Poof!* Up in smoke."

He leaned toward us.

"And that's not the worst part. She makes off with some money, you know? And some other stuff. So I'm trying to find her before anyone else does, because no one's real happy with her right now. She stole from the wrong sort of people."

"So you just sailed up to Galveston looking for her? What brought you here?"

"Well, Meagan told a friend she might stop in here. I think maybe she has an old boyfriend here. I'm not real clear on it. I don't know his name or what he does, but this girl Trish said she thought Meagan was going to see him. He lives in a little town up Highway 6 a ways. I don't put much stock in what Trish says, because she's a cokehead from way back. She's not all there, you know? Still, it's about all I've got to go on."

"Meagan — is that your girlfriend's name?"

"Yeah, but she'd be dumb to use it. I think she knows some people are looking for her. Wanna see a picture of her? Maybe you've seen her around. I've been asking everybody."

Brian, a thick guy with sun-bleached hair and the kind of tan that comes only from spending a week or so at sea, went below again. This time he came back with an 8 x 10 glossy of Margaret — the same shot Singer had retrieved from her motel room. David remarked on the quality of the shot, obviously done in a studio with some quality equipment.

"Yeah, some photographer guy did it as a favor to my boss," Brian said. "He did sessions with all the girls. My boss used them in advertisements, I guess."

"What are you doing now that you're here?"

"I work a few hours a day at the marina here," he said. "I do a lot of work on inboard diesel engines for the larger boats. It's hard work, but it pays for my slip fee, my rent-a-car, and some food now and then. I get electricity here free."

I nodded; rebuilding a diesel engine is hot, dirty work. I wouldn't want to do it on a boat, with access to the engine so limited and the space cramped. Brian seemed like a nice enough guy. He also seemed intelligent. If he'd just tried to murder Maggie, would he be telling his story to a couple of journalists? I doubted it.

"That's not a bad story," I said. "Now I'm sorry we can't print it, but I'll tell you what — if I see this girl, I'll tell her where to find you."

"Do more than that, if you can," Brian said sincerely. "I think she's in danger. Get her over here quick. I'm making the rounds, though; I'm checking the bars. I figure she only knows how to do one thing, so she'll be back at it soon. It's quick money — a real temptation for that kind of girl."

"Doesn't sound like you hold out much hope for her," I said.

"Her? No, my only obligation to her is to tell her they're looking for her. If she wants to come with me wherever I decide to go, she's welcome. If not, I've done my duty. But when she ran out on me, she proved she's not worth the time I'd spend trying to save her from herself, you know? If you're going to spend that kind of time trying to save someone, they'd better be worth the effort."

I looked over at David; he appeared as confused as I felt. Brian seemed sincere. He also corroborated Sally Nix's story. The only story we hadn't gotten was Margaret's.

"We'd better head out," I said. "Deadlines, you know."

David and I stood and walked back onto the dock, looking back. "Thanks for the Coke. Good luck finding this girl."

"I don't know if that would be good luck or not," Brian said, getting back to cleaning his boat.

David and I walked back to the car in silence. When we reached it, he threw his gear in the backseat and we got in.

"What more do we know now, Emerson?"

"Not much," I said. "Somebody's lying, and we don't know who. Someone's got about $50,000 and probably about a kilogram of cocaine. Margaret doesn't seem to have it on her; but then, she *was* packing a rather dangerous pistol that I'd never seen before."

"She had a gun?"

"Yeah. I startled her this morning, and she whipped it out like a pro. She had a round chambered and had it aimed at my head before I knew she was awake."

David started laughing. I didn't see what was so funny about the whole thing.

"Emerson, how do you get yourself in these places? If the dancer doesn't shoot you, Remington will. You do remember that tomorrow is her birthday?"

"Yes, I remember. How come everybody but me knows this? Did she tell you?"

"No. She made a bet with Ruth that you'd forget."

"Such faith in me. Did you talk to Ruth?"

"This morning. Remington must have called her as soon as she got to work. So Ruth calls, asks about the blonde."

"What did you tell her?"

"That I'm a dumb photographer and I don't know nothing."

"Wise move. I wish I was as smart as you."

"So what do we do now?"

"We talk to Mordechai. See if he's learned anything from Margaret."

About half an hour later we pulled into Mordechai's parking lot. In addition to the new Buick, there was a Jeep — but not the old army kind, the new slick kind that has probably never seen real mud in its life.

We entered the store and saw Mordechai on his stool behind his counter. For only having been open for two days, he seemed quite comfortable. He looked up at us and smiled.

"Did you catch any fish?"

"A small one," I said. "We found your boy. He's telling a better story than Maggie is at this point. Where is she, by the way?"

"Maggie is in the back. Go and see her."

He turned his attention back to a diamond he was placing into a ring. I felt a cold chill when I saw the diamond, and I almost shivered when I looked at the ring. Must have been the air conditioning vent.

We walked around the counter/display case and toward a back room, separated from the front by an old curtain. David pulled the curtain aside, and I followed him back. In the room I saw Margaret (or Maggie, I'd have to find out which she preferred) sitting at a table, drinking a cup of coffee.

With my guardian angel.

The mysterious Ms. Tate smiled up at me when she recognized me.

"Mordechai tells me you chose sapphires," she said. "Good choice. I'm sure she'll love them."

This must be Mordechai's "lady friend," I deduced astutely. I was amazed. She looked about the same — big hair, bright red nails, and the same laugh-lines around her eyes. The more I studied them, the more I liked them. She was a disarming person; if Margaret was going to open up to anyone, it would be Ms. Tate.

"You should have seen the deal he gave me," I said.

"I hope he was fair," she said. "If he wasn't, he'll hear from me."

Ms. Tate was probably about to say something else, but then we were all distracted.

The sound of several shotgun blasts destroying the front windows was a sound a little hard to ignore.

6

We could hear the glass being blown into the store. I thought of Mordechai, sitting up on his stool facing those windows. But while I thought, David acted.

David, who had been standing behind me, hit the floor, somehow taking me and Margaret with him. Luckily I broke the fall with my face. He was a little gentler on Margaret.

OK, so this was an unexpected twist. Not half as unexpected as what I saw next. Ms. Tate had an extremely large automatic pistol out and was diving for the bottom of the curtain. She rolled to the left as soon as she cleared it, keeping low and behind the counter. I heard Mordechai talking softly to her, but he sounded all right.

"They're gone," Ms. Tate said. "Everyone up."

We obeyed and walked slowly out to the front of the shop. Mordechai had been behind the counter and was fine. Margaret was expressionless. Ms. Tate was putting the large gun back into her purse. She looked up at me, and I didn't see any laugh-lines. I also didn't see the flighty, slightly pushy cosmetics salesperson I'd taken her for.

"Dunn, call the police," she said. "David, take my car and get Margaret out of here. Watch for anyone following you. Drive for at least thirty minutes before stopping anywhere. Now, do we have any ideas on a safe house?"

I got my keys from my jeans pocket.

"David, you know the new house?" I asked. He'd helped me move a few boxes over to the farmhouse I'd be renting starting next month. It was empty, and my new landlord told me to go ahead and start dropping stuff by. The electricity and water were working, but under the landlord's name. I was going to switch them over to my own name at the end of the month. The house had an old couch and a couple of chairs and a working refrigerator and stove. It would do for now. I tossed my new house key to David. Mordechai wrote down the address of the house as I dictated, and he said he or Sarah would be out there soon. David nodded, checked the front for any signs of anyone carrying a shotgun or a pipe bomb, then took off with Margaret in tow.

I reached for the phone and called the police. It was a 911 system, so they had the address as soon as they answered the phone. The dispatcher said a squad car would be by in a couple of minutes. I also suggested she send Singer.

As I hung up, I turned back around to face Mordechai and Ms. Tate. Both knew better than to get a broom and start sweeping yet; the cops would want everything to remain as is until the evidence guys arrived.

"OK, guys, how are we going to explain Margaret's involvement?"

"We won't. She was never here," Ms. Tate answered.

I'd had a bad night, I hadn't gotten much sleep, and furthermore guns were becoming an integral part of my life, and that was making me nervous. I might have been a little cranky, I admit.

At any rate angry words exploded out of my brain. "Look, Ms. Tate, just who are you? Some kind of renegade real estate agent? And what are you doing running around with a cannon and giving orders?"

"Later. And call me Sarah. Ms. Tate sounds so formal."

The cops arrived; Singer was not happy. Since gunshots were

involved, they sent the EMS around too. The paramedics took one look, saw that we were unhurt, and left.

"Let's go over this again," Singer said to Mordechai. "You've been open two days, and someone you don't know drives by and makes your showroom into an open-air porch. And you saw nothing."

"Yes."

"Then you've got great reflexes, buddy. Look at these."

He pointed to the wall just above Mordechai's stool — where holes left by buckshot pocked the plaster.

Mordechai shrugged, took his handkerchief, and wiped his forehead. He was still wearing his prayer shawl and hat. Did he even take them off to sleep? I wondered.

A patrol officer came into the store, carrying a plastic sandwich bag. It contained four spent shotgun shells. Sloppy work; I would have guessed a pro would clean up after himself. Singer took the bag, told the officer to have them kept as evidence, and turned back to me.

"Dunn, I hope you know what you're getting mixed up in. If all this ties back to the girl . . ."

"I don't know anything, Bill. As soon as I do, I'll call you. Believe me. But remember, this store's former owner and his associates were a bit prejudiced against Jews. This could have been some of them."

Actually the store's former owner probably had no prejudices; he was a slimebag to everyone on an equal-opportunity basis. But his workers were the kind of neo-Nazis who keep their barbers busy (skinheads, or "skins" as they call themselves). Most of the principal players in that recent adventure were cooling their heels in a Harris County jail cell awaiting the slow wheels of justice (which I expected would roll right over the creeps), but some of the hangers-on might be out for a little revenge. I mean, hey, it was a theory. Not a good one, but a theory.

"Maybe," Singer seemed to agree. "Or maybe you're getting yourself into the middle of an organized crime war. Dunn, Sally

Nix sent a message for you. She said to bail out. *Now.* She said to dump the blonde."

"I don't think I can, Bill."

Singer nodded. He knew more than he was letting on; he'd never let me off that easy if he didn't. Usually he'd order me to his office and threaten to lock me up just for being anywhere near an incident like this.

After about an hour of quality time with the city's finest, the last squad car left, and Singer's unmarked was close behind them. The clock on the wall read 6 P.M. I figured it was a good time for the nice middle-aged couple I'd met to come clean.

"You said you'd explain yourself later," I said to Sarah as Mordechai began sweeping up the glass that had been blown into his store. "It's later."

"There's not much you need to know."

"I need to know why I'm involved in this."

"You weren't involved in this until Sally Nix got you involved. If you have questions, ask her."

"She isn't here, but you are. So what's the deal? Are you a cop?"

"No," she said. "I'm anything but a cop. Just say I'm a free-lancer."

"That doesn't explain the gun."

"The gun? *My* gun?"

"I thought I recognized the make. Desert Eagle?"

"Good eye."

The Desert Eagle, an Israeli-made automatic loader, was just starting to grow in popularity here. It was already popular with certain Israeli elements, such as Israeli Defense Force officers.

"We're not getting very far, are we?" I asked.

Mordechai spoke up. "Emerson, you're a good boy. A dependable boy. But you ask too many questions. I'll drive you to your car. We'll talk a little then. But don't be so suspicious of Sarah."

I followed Mordechai to his new Buick and got in. He started it up, and we rolled out of the parking lot toward the newspaper office.

"Emerson, there are some bad people here."

"Present company excluded?"

He grinned. "Mostly. But the people here, they're up to no good. Maybe we can help, maybe no. But we must try. Your job is to keep safe. You're a good boy. This isn't your business. Maybe you should do what the lady detective says: bail out."

"Mordechai," I said nicely and politely, "not a chance. I don't know what's going on, but I will. And meanwhile, there's a girl someone's trying to kill. I want to know why. They say it's money, or maybe drugs. Maybe she stole something, maybe she did everything they said; that's what everyone — at least the people who know her — seem to believe. And I haven't ruled it out."

"Just be careful, my young friend," he said. "And keep David with you."

He pulled up to the newspaper's front door. I got out of the car.

"See you for dinner on Friday, yes?"

"Sure," I said. "See you then."

I didn't bother to go into the office, but got into my own car and drove home. I stayed only long enough to grab a Bible, then drove back through town toward the church.

Remington's car wasn't there yet when I pulled in; services didn't start until 7 P.M., about fifteen minutes later, and I was anxious to talk to Martin — alone.

Martin Paige, the pastor of Mill Valley Bible Church, had known me for almost ten years. He'd baptized me, he'd taught me about my new faith, and he'd put up with the growing pains I went through. Time after time I'd fall, but he never seemed to notice the mud or the scuff marks. Maybe he was just pretending not to, but even that was worth something to me.

I went into the foyer and around the hallway to the pastor's office. Martin was seated behind his desk, staring at a computer screen.

"I know that look," he said without looking at me. "What's her name?"

"Margaret. But that's not half the story."

"So I would assume. Your stories are never short, so you'd better get started."

He smiled as he turned his full attention to me. His hair was starting to show distinguished streaks of gray, but his clear eyes and thoughtful face were warm enough to soothe even the most distrustful souls. (I should know, I was one of them.) He was wearing his dark blue suit but didn't have his tie on yet.

I tried to tell him a condensed version of my tale, and about ten minutes later I looked into his eyes for an answer.

"What's your first impulse?" he asked.

"Dump her, get out of it, tell her to take a hike," I said. "She probably stole the money and drugs, and they're out to settle the score. Besides, she's an exotic dancer. Bad news. Bad news all around."

"And your second impulse?"

"Well . . . I guess to do what I can to protect her. What do you think I should do?"

"What if she's telling you the truth?"

I thought about that. "Then I guess it would be my duty to help as much as I could. If she really wants out of that business, that is."

"And what are the chances of that?"

"Pretty slim, I'd guess. But I'm cynical."

"I've noticed that about you. But do this: take a look at another situation. Take a kid who'd been on and off various drugs for about four years; he couldn't hold down a job, and he just wasn't someone you'd put a lot of stock in. Would you trust him? Take him into your home? Let him baby-sit your kids?"

I smiled. Martin had done exactly that (except I'm sure my innate charm showed through despite the rough edges). And it was mainly his sincerity, and the risk he took, that convinced me that maybe this church thing wasn't so bad after all.

"Take a chance," Martin said. "What's the alternative? Help only those we think deserve help? Save only those we think are worth saving?"

His words echoed something I'd heard earlier in the day. Brian seemed to think he should do exactly that — save someone only if that person is worth saving.

"That's not how Christ handled it," Martin said. Then he grinned. "But you knew that already."

A few minutes later Martin and I walked into the sanctuary. The pews were starting to fill, and I saw Remington a few rows back. I walked over to her and sat down beside her.

"Nice day at the office?" she asked.

"Nope. I didn't go into the office much. I met Margaret's ex-boyfriend, a few of us got shot at, and I learned my guardian angel packs a .44 Magnum. But other than that, I had a decent day. How about yours?"

"Not bad. Not as exciting as yours. Where's Margaret now?"

"She's with David at my new place. Oh no, I forgot again to tell the landlord I'm leaving. He's going to be heartbroken."

"She's in some serious trouble, Emerson. I checked with a friend at the Associated Press. There's a lot more going on down in Corpus Christi than just an exotic dancer running off with some money and drugs. There's an all-out gang war. And the owner of the bar where Margaret worked seems to be right in the middle of it."

Thanks for the information; we might need to check that out. I don't see how she could be involved in that, but maybe she's a bit-player."

The organist started up, and we went into the first hymn of the service. A couple more and a prayer or two later, Martin began his lesson; Wednesday nights he liked to have in-depth Bible studies.

He was a short way into the book of Psalms, teaching verse by verse. He was up to Psalm 22, the psalm which accurately prophesied Christ's suffering on the cross.

"It's a simple switch-out," Martin said. "Him for us. Substitution. The first part of the psalm tells of His pain. That would have — should have — been our pain.

"Then verse 24 gives us the why: 'For he hath not despised nor abhorred the affliction of the afflicted; neither hath he hid his face from him; but when he cried unto him, he heard.' He took our pain because we asked. We cry out, and He hears."

Martin seemed to be looking right at me as he spoke. I got the point. Margaret had asked for help.

After the Bible study, Remington walked me to my car.

"So what's the plan for tonight? Will Margaret need a place to sleep?"

"No," I answered. "We've got her at my new house just outside of town. David's been with her all afternoon. I'll go by and pick up the night shift, I guess. Maybe it would be better if Sarah Tate was there also."

"Don't worry. I trust you."

"It hadn't occurred to me that you wouldn't."

She laughed. "You're all alike. OK — call if you need anything. And I'll see you tomorrow night."

She kissed me and left.

I got into my car and headed west on Border Street toward F.M. 201. I went south on the farm-to-market road, informally called "Miller Road" since the only people who live on it are the Millers. It was still just a farm road. A few more miles and I arrived at the farmhouse I'd soon be living in — provided, of course, that I remained with the living. Two cars were parked in front — David's and Sarah Tate's. I wondered how David's car had gotten there if he had taken Sarah's. She must have driven it there.

The house was set back from the road about fifty yards. A few scrubby trees obscured the view a little, but I could tell that some lights were on inside. Only the backyard was fenced; a dirt driveway led up to the house in the front. David's car was behind Sarah Tate's Jeep.

The white, wood-frame building had been built long before air conditioning, but it was diagonally positioned so that no one side would get the full brunt of the morning or afternoon sun. It also had large, wide windows and a porch that went all the way around the two-bedroom house. The windows were for opening, and the porch was for settin'. That's a southern habit, not to be confused with sitting. Settin' involves much more, requiring a comfortable chair (preferably a rocking chair or a swing) and a fondness for doing nothing. I planned to do quite a bit of it when I moved in at the end of the month.

I parked behind David's car and went onto the porch.

Sarah Tate, my big-haired guardian angel, opened the door as I walked up to it.

"Good — you're here. This is a nice house."

"Yeah, well, it's not officially mine until the first of the month."

"It is now. I called the owner — such a nice elderly man — and let him know you'd need it a little sooner. The telephone company will also turn your service on here within a few days. They couldn't tell me exactly when, but you know how they are."

"Why do I suddenly feel that I'm not in control here?"

I heard David laugh. "You haven't been in control since you started dating Remington."

His laugh sounded not unlike an iguana being dribbled downcourt. Thoughts of violence crossed my mind.

"You're one to talk," I said, brushing by Sarah to reconsider that earlier decision I made to not punch my best friend. "You're almost completely trained now. Ruth has you saying, 'Yes, ma'am' and 'No, ma'am' and using every piece of silverware they give you at the restaurant."

The living room of the house was large and barren. The owner had repainted recently, so mixed in with that musty old-house smell was the clean scent of fresh latex. The hardwood floors were clean also. The one couch and two dining chairs were arranged along opposite walls, and a blow-up mattress with a couple of sleeping bags had been placed to the side of the room. The kitchen, off to my right, now had a card table in it. Grocery bags were atop the card table, and I felt certain the refrigerator was stocked. To my left was the hallway leading to the bedrooms; it was dark, but I could see the bedroom doors were shut.

David was slouching on one of the chairs — looking comfortable on a stiff, straight-back dining chair as only he could — while Margaret was reading a magazine on the couch. When I came in, she put the magazine down and looked up at me; she almost looked relaxed.

"Hi, Emerson."

"Hi, Maggie. Is it Maggie or Margaret? Or maybe even Meagan, if you're more comfortable with that."

"Now, I think, it's Maggie."

"What's the plan?" I asked, since I was already out of the decision-making process.

"Simple," Sarah said. "I stay here with Maggie. We'll get along just fine."

"But if someone's trying to kill her, can you take care of her? I think maybe David or I should —"

"Don't worry about her," David said, rising from the chair quickly. He grabbed his ever-present camera bag and my arm and led me toward the door.

"OK, Sarah, we'll see you later," he said.

"Wait," I said, my irritation showing. "They're going to be sitting ducks here. We need to stay. They don't even have a phone yet."

Sarah smiled and walked into the kitchen, getting her purse. Instead of a huge gun, this time she pulled out a small cellular phone.

"I have David's beeper number, so if we need you, we'll call," she said gently. "You boys go on home and forget about us. We'll be just fine."

"Emerson . . ." came Maggie's voice as I was being led from my own house. "I need to talk to you — not now, but sometime. Can you come back tomorrow night, after work?"

"He's got a date," David said, still leading me out. "With his fiancée."

The door slammed shut behind us just before I turned to David. The thought of a quick, painful strangulation occurred to me. To make things worse, he was grinning. "Oops. I didn't mean fiancée — not yet anyway," he said.

"Don't rush me to the altar," I said, leaning against the porch railing. "Now tell me what's up. Why are you so ready to leave Maggie with someone we just met?"

"I don't know, Emerson. But I do know one thing: Sarah is not just a little old lady. My uncle ordered me to ask no questions. That means one thing to me. No questions."

"Mossad maybe?"

"You saw her gun. Imagine the way she can use it. What do you think? I don't make any assumptions, but if my uncle says to trust her, I trust her."

I had to admit the old gal was quick on the trigger. And few realtors I knew carried Desert Eagles in their handbags. Her being in the Israeli secret service would explain a lot; the problem was, it raised about ten questions for every one it answered.

"Emerson, I don't think it's a good idea for us to get more involved than we have to."

"I think we're already involved," I said.

I walked to my car and opened the door. I turned back to David. "Does this mean Mordechai . . ."

He shrugged. "I don't know," he said. "Mordechai was very important. Now he comes here."

David looked a little troubled.

"Emerson, you know it took eighteen months for the paperwork to go through for me to come here. Mordechai comes with less than a week's notice. Maybe he has drinking buddies in the government, I don't know."

"And that was a quick sale on the business," I said. "He doesn't seem much interested in turning a profit either. Think he's Mossad too?"

"I was ordered not to ask. He's the closest thing to a father I've known. He's also a colonel. So I obey. But I think Maggie is safe. I also think she's got the hots for you."

"Got the hots for me? You're joking. I've only known her for three days."

"She kept asking about you. I kept telling her about Remington."

"Thanks. I'm sure Remington will appreciate that. Since when were you on her side anyway?"

"Since I realized it is better for us to surrender with dignity. Our defeat, my friend, is assured. Ruth, as you say, has me trained."

"Go home, and when you call her, make sure you tell her I

made no lip contact with any blondes tonight. That way I know it will get back to Remington."

"OK, Emerson. See you."

He was behind me most of the way back into town. Once we got onto Commerce Street, he went off to the east and I went west to my apartment. It was after 10:00, so I scribbled out a note to my landlord explaining that I'd be moving in a couple of weeks. My lease had expired long ago, and I was on a month-to-month deal now, so two weeks was enough notice. I walked over and left the note in the Ewens' mailbox; they had my work number, so if they wanted to gripe, they could call me in the morning. I doubted they would; they were in their eighties and had seen dozens of renters come and go. I walked back up my own stairs. I didn't think I'd miss this place — not much, at least. And it would be great to get Airborne down here. I missed that certain something that only a long-haired dog can add to one's life: namely, the inability to wear dark colors.

I went into my apartment and saw the light blinking on my answering machine. I hit the Play button.

"Emerson, this is Sally Nix. I can't tell you where I'm calling from, but you need to know something. If you're not smart enough to get out of this with your skin intact, which I doubt you are, then you'd better at least start looking in the right place: Club Paradise, Nueces County. Be discreet. And don't get yourself killed. A man named Maxwell is the one to look out for. Take care of yourself — and if you still believe her, take care of Meagan — Margaret Sullivan. I thought she was using me, but now I'm not so sure."

The message ended there; it only added to my confusion.

8

That night I lay awake thinking things over.

On Monday a beautiful blonde walks into my boring life and adds a little excitement. Or at least interest. On Tuesday her car gets blown up into little bitty pieces. On Wednesday we meet her ex-boyfriend, and an hour later Mordechai's new store is shot up. Then a big-haired old lady who tips well turns out to possibly be Israeli intelligence.

Not a bad week, altogether.

I dropped off to sleep thinking about Maggie; she was the key. The only problem was, we couldn't find the right lock. Or at least I couldn't.

Maybe the answer was at Club Paradise.

The next thing I knew it was morning, light was coming in from my window, and I heard the telephone ringing. I reached under my bed, pulled out Sarah Tate's Desert Eagle, and shot it until it stopped.

Or maybe I dreamed that part. At any rate, the ringing stopped. As I came to full consciousness, I saw no holes in the phone, and the receiver was in my hand, so I assumed the part about the gun was a product of my overworked imagination.

"Hello?" I said, closing my eyes against the morning light.

"Who is this?" came a cautious female voice I didn't recognize.

"What? You called me. You should know."

"I'm looking for Meagan. She there? Do you know her?"

"Meagan?"

"Sorry, I must have the wrong number. Sorry. Good-bye."

"No! Wait!" I shouted. "I know her. She's not here now, but I know where she is. You need to talk to her?"

The woman paused. I could sense indecision at the other end of the line. "Yeah . . . I need to talk to her. It's important. Can you give me her number?"

"She's not at a phone," I said. "Can I take a message to her?"

"Who is this?" she asked again.

"I'm a friend. Where did you get this number?"

"Some of Meagan's stuff. From her locker at work. I need to find her."

"You mentioned that. Is she in trouble? Are you in trouble?"

"Her. I can't talk about it to you. I don't know you. My name is Trish. Tell her to call Trish. Leave a message at the bar. I probably won't be there, but I'll get the message."

"All right. I'll tell her. Anything else you want me to tell her?"

"No."

"All right, then — my name is Dunn — Emerson Dunn. If you need to contact her again, call me here. Or at the office. I work at the *Times*, the local newspaper."

The telephone went dead. I put it down and stared up at the ceiling. A warning call from someone named Trish. I could figure out the warning she would like to give Maggie: Watch out for pipe bombs and shotgun blasts.

I got up and showered. I grabbed a bagel on my way out the door. I knew enough to realize it was Thursday, Aggie Catherine Remington's birthday.

I drove to the office, a shabby building that smelled like newsprint and perfume (from the ad reps) and coffee. Sharon was at her desk and grinning as I went in.

"Don't even start," I said. "Yes, I know today is Remington's birthday. Yes, I've got dinner reservations. What more do you women want from me?"

"Complete obedience," Sharon said. The forty-six-year-old had spent most of her life keeping a husband and three kids in line. She was a big woman, so I bet she did a good job of it.

I went to my desk. Robert was already in. I started sifting through the mail, and a few minutes later Sherri walked in.

"Hi, chief," she said, going to her desk, the one closest to Sharon. I think she picked that one out of fear that David, Robert, and I might gang up on her. The reality of it was that she and Sharon ganged up on the whole lot of us.

"Morning. OK, everyone, what's today?"

"Remington's birthday," Robert and Sherri said in unison.

"I hope you remembered to get her something," Sherri said. "If my boyfriend didn't, I'm afraid I couldn't be held accountable for my actions."

Tough talk for a somewhat mousy twenty-one-year-old. She was just out of college, still seeing her high school prom date, and living at home with her parents over in Friendswood, about fifteen minutes away. Sherri's shoulder-length strawberry-blonde hair was completely natural, and she wore little makeup. You got the feeling that she was a no-nonsense student. She ran the high school newspaper her senior year, then worked on her college newspaper at Houston Baptist University. She edited that her last semester.

Sherri's real strength was feature writing. People like to read about other people, not just city council meetings. She was a good complement to Robert, who loved politics. He'd eat up the infighting and the backstabbing that was always present on the council; he could sift through it and come up with the real issues and the real problems. I was helping him learn to write about it so the average reader would care as much as he did. To do that, you always say what effect it's going to have on police protection and on the tax rate. In a small town, that's about all anyone cares about.

"What are you guys working on?" I asked, just to get an idea of what the Sunday paper was going to look like.

"They're putting the budget together over at City Hall, and it's not looking good," Robert said. "Probably at least a 5 percent tax hike just to keep city services level with this year."

I grinned. Robert was getting the hang of it. I liked Robert; he was a little older than Sherri, but also just out of college. He'd gone to Sam Houston State University. He'd worked his way up to sports editor on that school's newspaper but wanted out of sports. I gave him a shot, and he was proving to be a competent hard-news reporter.

I take that back. He was turning out to be a darn good reporter, period. Within a year or so, he'd be as good as I was. That probably bothered me a little more than I cared to admit. But Robert was a good guy. He worked well with David on the spot-news (that's when you rush out to the scene of a fire or an accident — a car bombing, for example), and I was starting to teach him the principles of layout. I wanted to make him assistant editor in a year or so.

Sherri said she had a piece on the school district's budget too, but was working harder on an article on recruiting minority teachers.

"That sounds interesting," I said. "What are you finding out?"

"That we don't stand a chance," she said. "Minority teachers are at a premium. Some districts in Florida are coming over here and offering signing bonuses to graduates, just like football players. We need more minority teachers here, but we can't compete with that."

"Good story," I said. "What about art?"

"I set up a shoot for David — Mrs. Randall's summer Honors English class over at the high school. She's got twenty students, fifteen of whom are black or Hispanic. We can get a shot of the back of the kids' heads, showing a white teacher. Mrs. Randall won't mind; she's the chair of the minority recruitment committee."

"Do I even need to be here?"

"Nope," Robert grinned. "Except maybe to take the heat for

us. The mayor's going to be calling in a few minutes. He's not going to be happy about our story in today's paper — the one about him trying to talk the EPA out of citing the city for violations at the landfill."

I sighed. It had been a good article — about how the mayor got into an argument at a public meeting with a representative from the EPA. The mayor did come off looking a little pushy. But then, Mayor Sam, as he was known and had been known during all his twenty-two years in office, *was* a little pushy.

Later that morning I got the call, calmed the mayor down, and told him not to pick fights with the Feds anymore.

Louise had called a staff meeting for noon; when she did that she always brought in some lunch. So at noon we followed her into the break room and listened to the quarterly financial report. That part was more for the ad reps than for us. Then she got around to the editorial side. She gave us some pointers on how to handle the upcoming budget season without boring our readers to death, and she told us we'd be putting out a back-to-school issue in mid-August. She gave me a list of assignments to divvy up.

David showed up about five minutes into the meeting. He looked apologetically at Louise and helped himself to the lasagna she'd brought.

That afternoon I punched out an editorial on Mayor Sam's fight with the EPA, just to make my point a little clearer: Don't pick fights with people who can shut down your landfill and thereby nearly shut down your city.

As I read the editorial over one last time, I realized I was starting to think like a grown-up, to care about grown-up things. Scary thought. So I started playing with the Mr. Potato Head in my desk, just to keep things in perspective.

At about 3 P.M. I called the restaurant. Walter answered. Everything was in order, he said; our table would be ready at 7:45.

I ran across the street to the drugstore and found some wrapping paper. After I botched the wrapping job a couple of times, Sherri kindly helped me out.

"These are beautiful," she said of the necklace and earrings. "I approve."

"Thanks. I got a deal on them. Although I don't think I want to get into the habit of getting her jewelry."

"Don't worry," Sharon piped up. "There's only one more piece of jewelry that counts anyway."

I threw a crumpled mess of wrapping paper (from my first attempt) at her and went back to supervising Sherri.

"Much obliged," I said as she finished. "I couldn't have done it without you."

"You're right."

I went back to my desk and called Remington.

"You've lost your bet with Ruth," I said. "I'll pick you up at your place at 7:30."

"Fine. What should I wear?"

"Something nice."

I didn't tell her we were merely going to a gas station-turned restaurant for the evening. I was sure Walter and Gunther would go all-out to make the evening nice.

A few hours later I drove home before heading to Remington's apartment near the community college. I called Mordechai to make sure everything with Sarah and Maggie was, well, kosher and asked him to relay the message from Trish.

Mordechai was a little leery of the message; he asked if I knew how Trish had gotten my number. I told him what she'd said, about finding it among other items in Maggie's locker at the bar. He seemed satisfied and said he'd tell Maggie.

I put on my nicest suit (the only one I didn't pick out myself) and headed over to Remington's.

As I pulled into a parking space just below her apartment, it started to rain. I grimaced and jogged up the flight of stairs to her door. She answered at the first knock.

"Good timing. But if it's raining, I'm not riding around in that colander of yours," she said, kissing me lightly. "We'll take my car. It doesn't leak."

Remington lacked any respect at all for my car; its main function in life was lugging my sailboat over to Clear Lake or Offats Bayou on Galveston Island. She liked sailing well enough, once she became convinced that I wasn't out to drown her and that it's natural for a sailboat to lean to one side a little (it's called heeling over). But she had no appreciation for the fine automobile that made all of that possible. Could David's little Toyota haul that sailboat thirty miles? I think not. It takes a huge, environmentally hostile V-8 engine and a heavy tank of a car to do the job.

Somehow Remington couldn't get past the fact that the twenty-year-old car had flaking, sky-blue paint and rust around some admittedly important areas, such as the door hinges, and that the heater didn't work in the winter. And it had a few leaks — only around the windshield and the windows and the roof and the doors.

I was smart enough to know that no single driveway would ever be big enough for Remington's car and that Ford of mine. Another good reason to refrain from buying too much jewelry.

Remington gave herself one last once-over in her bedroom mirror. As she came out of her bedroom, I took her hand.

"You look wonderful," I said. "Gorgeous — but somehow incomplete."

She frowned a little. I dropped her hand and reached for my suit coat pocket. The clock read 7:35. My timing was impeccable.

"One thing you lack," I said. I fumbled around in my pocket and eventually pulled out the gift-wrapped necklace and earrings.

"Happy birthday." I put the necklace on her from behind, just like they do in those commercials.

Only I realized that once again real life doesn't imitate commercials. The first thing she did was take off the necklace so she could look at it. She made the appropriate noises, and then I had to put the necklace back on her. Then she went straight to the bathroom to stare at it in the mirror.

The whole thing took about five minutes of my life. Then we went through the same thing (approximately) with the earrings, although she put those on herself. Another three minutes of my life.

"I love them," she said, grabbing my neck and squeezing.

I felt the goosebumps rise on the back of my neck. I mean, she was one syllable from saying the dreaded Three Little Words. I sincerely hoped she wouldn't ruin a perfectly nice night with that sort of seriousness.

"Our dinner awaits," I said. She followed me onto the landing in front of her apartment.

She locked her door, then handed me the keys.

"You drive," she said.

I nodded. I unlocked her side of the car, then got in myself. I tried to stay as dry as possible, but it wasn't really working. Once inside the car, I realized she was probably right; she looked too nice to get drenched in my car on the way over to the restaurant.

"Did you have any help picking these out?"

Trick question. *Watch yourself, Dunn.*

"Well, of course not," I said. "Not much anyway. And it was from a little old lady, so there."

"No help from a blonde with bright red lipstick?"

"None whatsoever."

"Then who wrapped it? Remember, I had to wrap your mother's birthday present."

"Sherri helped a little."

"Thank her for me."

"You bet."

We drove the rest of the way in silence. That's a valuable thing, to be comfortable enough with someone that neither of you feels like one of you has to be talking. Remington reached over and took my right hand.

We pulled into the parking lot and parked close to the

entrance. I took the umbrella and got out first, then opened Remington's door for her.

The doors were locked as we went up to the restaurant. I knocked as we stood sheltered under the small awning — and I was a little shocked when Walter opened the door. He was wearing a tuxedo. So was Gunther.

"Your table is ready," Walter said, bowing stiffly.

Remington stifled a snicker as I led her into the darkened diner. The boys had gone all-out; there was only one table, and it had a real tablecloth. It even had real silverware!

"Might I be so bold as to say that your necklace is exquisite," Walter said crisply as Remington passed. I slyly motioned to my ear, and Walter quickly added "And those earrings as well. Lovely."

Such service.

Gunther pulled out the chair for Remington, but not for me; I was on my own.

"Your meal will be ready in a moment," he said. He and Walter then made the best possible use of themselves — they went into the kitchen.

"I think we're a little underdressed," she said, smiling. "Wanna place a small wager on when they'll start fighting?"

"That won't happen tonight, my dear. They'll be on their best behavior. Just watch."

"I'm watching. And listening. We'll hear pots within five minutes."

"You're on."

We talked about work and David and Ruth and her parents and my dog for a while, and it was getting harder and harder to ignore the rising Germanic voices coming from the kitchen. I told her about Sally's message on my machine. Remington nodded.

"If nothing else, Maggie's worth giving the benefit of the doubt," I said. "I need to find out more about this boyfriend. Maybe that would be the best thing for her, to sail away with him to the Bahamas or Belize or somewhere like that. Somewhere people won't be bombing her car. I really think —"

A loud clang stopped me mid-sentence, and Remington looked at her watch.

"That's another $1 million you owe me. That makes it about $60 million so far, I think. This relationship is costing you some serious money."

I nodded. Boys will be boys. A few moments later a slightly flustered Walter emerged from the kitchen.

"I am sorry, but we must wait on the potatoes. I feel they were not up to our high standards, so we are preparing them new."

"No problem, chef," I said. "We're enjoying the ambiance of the joint."

Walter again bowed and returned to the kitchen.

"Do you know how old I am?" Remington asked with a deceptive casualness, deftly changing the subject from the blonde to her birthday.

It was another trick question. I hate these.

"Of course I do. You're twenty-six."

"Was that an answer or a question?"

"An answer. And if I'm wrong, just tell me. Soon. The suspense is killing me."

"No, you're right. I was just making sure."

"Making sure of what?"

"That you're paying attention."

Dames.

Walter emerged a few minutes later with our meal — Gunther's jaegerschnitzel with Walter's potatoes. They left us to eat alone, but I kind of missed them. I think hearing their German accents somehow enhances the flavor of the food.

Over dinner we talked a little more about the Sunday school class; Remington said that one of the girls was starting to skip more and more Sundays, and she'd heard the girl was having trouble in school. Remington said she'd try to get the girl alone

Sunday morning — if she showed — and find out if anything was wrong.

"Oh, wait," I said. "I almost forgot something. We're invited to David's house for Sabbath dinner tomorrow night. Can you make it? Mordechai, David's uncle, is going to cook. It should be good."

"As if I would turn down an invitation like that," she said.

We were just finishing up when from somewhere deep inside the kitchen we heard the sound of a horn section. The boys had come through on the music. A Cole Porter beat came filtering through to the table, and I smiled as a silky baritone voice began singing something our parents had probably listened to.

"Sinatra," I said.

"I know that." Remington smiled.

"May I have this dance?"

Frank Sinatra sliced through the subtle tension as we danced in the area the boys had cleared out for that specific purpose. I wondered where the boys had found the music. Was Sinatra popular in Germany?

Remington laid her head on my shoulder and laughed. "I'm sorry to have been catty about Margaret," she said. "It's none of my business. I just get a little worried about us."

"What do you mean?"

"We don't see much of each other anymore, except at church. I don't think I've got a real good grip on what's going on. Something seems to be slipping away. I'm a little nervous, and maybe I'm a little jealous too."

"Me too."

"You too what?"

"All of that. Did I ever tell you I'm a little jealous of your job? You've really made it. And did I mention, by the way, that I'm proud of you?"

"No, you hadn't mentioned that." She held me a little tighter as we continued dancing.

"Well, I am. Very impressive. You don't mind dating a guy who's still stuck in a small-town job?"

"I wouldn't mind spending my life with a guy who's stuck in a small-town job."

I felt the back of my neck ice over. She'd said it. She'd alluded to it, at least. I paused in place. She moved a little away from me.

"I think dessert is on its way," I said, leading her back to the table by the hand.

She let go of my hand before we reached the table. She sat down unceremoniously and stared down at her plate.

"Oh my gosh, did I say that?" she asked.

"One of us did," I said. I couldn't see much of her face in the dim candlelight, but I knew her birthday date wasn't turning out as she had expected.

I reached over and touched her face.

"Me too," I said.

She paused a moment, then laughed.

"Me too? What's *that*? We've got a romantic candlelight dinner, Sinatra in the background, two psychochefs in the kitchen, and the best you can come up with is 'Me too'? I thought you were a writer, Dunn. You're supposed to be able to dazzle me with words. You've done it before."

I grinned. "Pretty weak, eh?"

She nodded. "I'd say so."

"OK," I said. "Then how about this: I love you."

Even Sinatra hushed for that one. Sudden silence followed my statement.

Her eyes got big, and she stared into my face, searching my eyes as hard as I was searching my soul.

"Well, yeah, I'd say that was an improvement."

"It's been a long time since I said that to anyone."

"I know."

I don't remember much about dessert. The boys came out with an apple cake loaded with candles. She blew them out and we ate it, all four of us. The boys had apparently called a temporary truce. As far as details, I could see little in front of me other than her face. Her dark shoulder-length hair framed it well; the sapphires did indeed look good against her skin.

The boys poked me in the ribs knowingly as we walked out, and I slipped them some money. I tried to find it in my heart to give them the benefit of the doubt, of course. Walter and Gunther were far too mature to eavesdrop. But *someone* had to have stopped Sinatra at that precise moment. I reminded myself to insult their schnitzel next time I was in.

It had stopped raining.

We walked to Remington's car, and she handed me the keys again. "You drive," she said.

"All right."

I unlocked her door and opened it for her, then went around to the driver's side. I got in and started the engine.

We drove without speaking again. We pulled into her complex, and I parked.

"What now?" I asked.

"You walk me to my door," she said.

"How gentlemanly of me."

I followed her to her door and handed her the keys. She stopped after she unlocked it.

"Hey, Dunn," she said as she turned to face me. "Me too."

And then she kissed me and went inside.

Friday went quickly; Robert and Sherri got their stories in on deadline (noon), and I had the inside pages pasted up by 3:00. David developed his photos and dropped them on my desk for me to tag and said dinner would be at about 8:00. I said we'd be there. I called Mordechai at 4:00, just to see if everything was OK.

"Of course, of course," he said. "You will come for dinner? We will talk more then."

"You bet we will. See you then."

The office cleared out by 5:30. I told Robert and Sherri to get out of Dodge, and David went on home to help Mordechai fend off the advice and help Rebecca would surely offer. It was, after all, her kitchen. I doubt she'd let those two lift a finger there without strict supervision.

Louise and I had the front page put together by 7:00, so all that was left to do was proofing it one last time before it was committed to eternal print.

Louise said she could handle it, so I called Remington and headed over to her place. When I arrived, it was a little awkward, as if neither of us was sure the other really meant what we'd said last night. But instead of the usual kiss hello, I got a long hug.

"Should we forget about last night?" she asked.

"Why would we do that? It was one of the best nights of my life," I said.

She looked up at me and smiled. "*That's* why I'm dating a writer. Keep it up."

We took her car again. On the way over to David's house, she asked about the theological implications of us two Christians having a Sabbath dinner with a houseful of Jews.

"I asked Martin about that once," I said. "He just looked at me funny and said that Jesus was a Jew. Martin didn't seem to think He would mind."

Remington nodded. I told her a little more about Mordechai. She'd heard me talk about him, but she hadn't met him yet. She was in for an experience.

A few minutes later we pulled up in front of David's house and parked.

"Do you get to wear a beanie?" she asked with a grin.

"Yup. It's called a yarmulke, though. Mordechai will probably be wearing a hat."

Rebecca greeted us at the door; she looked a little flustered.

"I should search you for cigars," she said as I walked in. She hugged me instead. "You should see the mess they make of my home, of my kitchen. A. C., you must help me. I cannot watch them all. Too many men!"

Remington smiled as she kissed our hostess on the cheek and said she'd do what she could to help control the bunch of us. We walked into the dining room. David and Carl were already at the table; Carl had a small glass with a clear liquid in it. I sat down beside him, leaving a place beside me for Remington.

"Emerson, try this," Carl said. "This is high-octane stuff. Mordechai brought it over; it's an Arab liquor called arak."

He handed me the glass. I looked at it, then took a sip. It was a small sip, but for about five minutes afterwards I couldn't feel my lips.

"None for me, thanks," I said. "You boys go ahead. But if you pull out the cigars around that, we'll all go up in flames."

"Jet fuel." David grimaced. "I'll take a Coke. Want one, Emerson?"

"Sure," I said. I was all for experiencing another culture, and the Jews had no moratorium on alcohol, but my innards told me I'd better stick with a soft drink.

Mordechai emerged, carrying platters from the kitchen. Rebecca and Remington helped, fearful that the big Israeli would drop something or do some other unspeakable damage.

"Emerson, good to see you," he said. "And your fiancée, she is so pretty. What does she see in you? Ah me, I know not what women are thinking of. For example, take my sister. Please."

He roared with laughter as Carl and David quickly joined him. I started to join in when Remington and Rebecca emerged with the cutlery. They hadn't heard Mordechai's exhumation of a long-dead joke, but they knew the boys were at it again. They eyed us suspiciously as they sat down.

David took a Hebrew Bible from a table in the corner. Carl handed out yarmulkes, and we stood. David read a few verses — in Hebrew, of course — and every so often Mordechai and Carl would say, "Amen," though it sounded like "Ah-main," and I had no idea when to join in. Then we sat down and ate.

Mordechai had prepared fish, as promised. As he had said, it was spicy. Remington handled it well, although she did drink a lot of water. There was also a kind of salad with raisins and carrots in it, a dish with peas, and several other foreign delicacies.

"Now, my young friend Emerson, we can talk," Mordechai said after a few minutes. "We are among family. David tells me you have a dog, yes?"

"Yes, up in Dallas," I said. "I'm going to bring him down as soon as I move into the farmhouse."

"But in a sense the farmhouse is already yours," Mordechai said. "I think it would not be a bad idea to have a dog even now. Is it a big dog, a protective dog?"

"Well, he's big, and he has a deep bark," I said. "Sure, he'd be good security. Should I get him this weekend?"

"I think maybe yes. And you must obtain something more. Information on Garrett Maxwell."

Remington's eyes widened a little. Maggie must have told her the name of her old boss.

"OK. I can drive up to Dallas and be back with Airborne by, say, 8 P.M. tomorrow. That would leave David and me all day Sunday to check out Nueces County. But what could we learn in just a few hours?"

"We'll know when we find it, I guess," David said.

I nodded. Remington looked a little apprehensive. She hadn't gotten used to the way Mordechai gave orders and everyone else seemed to obey.

"Mordechai, what do you expect us to find?" I asked.

He considered it for a moment and after apparently judging it a fair question offered an answer.

"Look for conflict; territorial probably."

That fit with what Remington had found out. There was a gang war or a drug war or maybe both going on.

Mordechai leaned over the table a little. "Look for one side to be winning."

"Why?"

Mordechai went back to eating, ignoring the question. We resumed the meal also. Apparently there was only so much information he was willing to divulge.

A few minutes later he looked up at me.

"Emerson! Why don't you eat?"

"I *am* eating. This is my second plateful."

"You are too skinny. It is good that you get married."

I almost choked. He didn't pause to check on my health.

"This is a very nice girl. She will be good to you. She will fatten you up. I had a wife once. Before that, I was skinny, just like you. But my wife, she fattens me up. Now I am like this. You believe me?"

"Sure," I said. "Where's your wife now?"

"She left me for a skinny man!" He howled with laughter

again, and Carl, obviously helpless around this bad influence, doubled over. David was snickering. His mother was staring straight at him, as if to say, "Don't fall in with this lot."

Rebecca leaned toward Remington.

"He never had a wife," she said. "He lies. I tried though. I bring home all my friends. And all my friends, they say, 'No way.' It is because he does not behave. So he never had a wife."

"It's not too late," Remington said. "Even the worst of them can be reformed."

She kicked me under the table for added emphasis.

"Well, I don't know about him," Rebecca said. "I've given up hope. And now all my friends are married. Ah, maybe some will be widows soon; then they might take a second look."

"Mordechai, these women will have you on the used-husband lot before we know it if we stay around here much longer," Carl said. "Come on out back on the deck. I want to show you that new barbecue grill."

Mordechai's face got serious, in deep contemplation of this new grill and exactly what technological wonders it would have. Yeah, right. These two weren't fooling anyone.

"Don't bother coming back inside if you smell like cigars," Rebecca said. "You just sleep out there. No cigars!"

Within five minutes all four of us men were out back on the deck. Wafting up into the atmosphere was the distinct aroma of fine cigars — Dunhills. Carl and Mordechai indulged; David and I just sat back and listened.

Carl and Mordechai were discussing some new oil fields being put into production in Israel. After a while David nudged me.

"What should I do about Ruth?"

"What do you mean?" I asked.

"I haven't seen her in almost two weeks."

"You still talk to her almost every day, right?"

"It's not the same."

"Yeah. I don't know what to tell you. If Remington didn't live here, I'd never see her either. Have you told Ruth you'd like to spend more time with her, or have you just been saying 'OK' whenever she says she's tied up?"

David looked a little indignant.

"I'm not going to force anyone to see me," he said. "I just say, 'OK, that's fine with me.' If she wants to see me, she will come. If no, then no."

"Meanwhile, you're letting a small problem grow into a major problem. Tell her how you feel. Tell her you miss her. Your mother didn't raise you to hide your feelings."

He grinned at that. His mother, who'd brought him up alone after her first husband died in the Six Day War, tended to lean the other direction. That is, she expressed herself no matter what. The unpleasant thought occurred to me that she'd be expressing her opinion in mere minutes, when she discovered that Carl had smuggled some cigars in.

Actually the cigars went back a ways with David and me. A few months before I started dating Remington, David and Ruth took it upon themselves to Find Emerson A Girl.

The first option, according to Ruth, was the herd of girls who'd made it through college with her without getting married. I should have known then to beware. My dorm mother once told me that anyone who couldn't find a mate in college was pretty likely doomed. "When else in your life are you going to live with several hundred single persons of the opposite sex?" she asked. And she had a point. The after-college dating scene wasn't pretty.

Not that some of these girls Ruth dug up weren't pretty. Some were. And maybe I wasn't as cooperative as I should have been. In fact, cigars played a key part in salvaging that time period in my life.

We called it the Churchill Gambit. When Ruth — a really sweet girl who meant nothing but good — would set up these Dates From The Bermuda Triangle (they could have been worse), David and I would prearrange a signal. Then, if the date turned out to be, well, wretched, we had an easy out.

A perfect example was this girl Ruth had met in a communications class. Her name was Laurie. By the time salad was brought to our table, Laurie was telling me all about her last five relationships and exactly which character flaws in her partners doomed the relationships to failure.

We were on Number 4, The Slob, when we reached an open-air porch to watch a band (the drummer had gone to a Christian college with me). I motioned to David, who sighed but reached into his ever-present photographer's vest (Ruth had yet to rid her life of that vest in her efforts to reform David). Out came cigars. We, of course, offered one to Laurie. She declined and looked on with horror as we proceeded to chase away all midsummer mosquitoes and most of the people at neighboring tables.

Within minutes Laurie found an excuse to have to go home, right away. She made no mention of seeing me again. Ruth later told me that I had offended one of her dearest friends (but she added that sometimes friends such as that *need* a little offending).

Martin didn't exactly approve of cigars as a pastime, but he said that was his opinion and he refused to draw any hard-and-fast lines on the issue; he just quoted the Apostle Paul as saying that while all things might be legal, not everything was beneficial. And Remington was beginning to put her foot down about it. However, every once in a while David and I would still sneak off. When older reprobates such as Carl and Mordechai fell in with us — or we with them — the women didn't stand a chance. But this close to Rebecca and her kitchen knives, David and I figured we'd better abstain.

I heard a door slam behind us, and I knew that despite our innocence on this occasion we were about to be busted anyway. The law of conspiracy. We knew of the crime and stood by while it was carried out; therefore we were accomplices.

"I knew it," Rebecca said. "You men."

Either she was too mad or too resigned to the situation to say anything more, so she stormed back into the house.

Mordechai started giggling, and pretty soon Carl, David, and I were doubled over with him.

"So, Emerson, you will go to get your dog tomorrow?" Mordechai asked, wiping his forehead with his handkerchief.

"Sure," I said. "I might as well. I hope my dad hasn't gotten too attached."

"You know, when I was a boy I wanted a dog," he said. "But she —"

He motioned at the door, meaning his big sister.

"She wouldn't let me," he said. "She told our mother I'd give it fleas."

That set us off again.

"David, his jokes are awful," I said a few moments later to my photographer and fellow journalist, my fellow seeker of truth. David nodded, acknowledging that in this case "awful" was indeed the truth.

"So why do we laugh?" I asked.

He looked a little confused. "Maybe because our own jokes aren't that great either."

"I can accept that."

Mordechai looked almost serious again.

"Emerson, I want you to take Maggie along with you. She can help you drive, and maybe she will talk to you."

"Hasn't she talked to Sarah? I thought she'd trust another woman."

Mordechai thought about it for a moment. "I think, Emerson, her former employment did not leave her in a position to trust women, or many men for that matter."

I had to agree. An exotic dancer would have to know that the mainstream of women would look down on her because of her job, even if the dancer herself considered it *only* a job and nothing more.

"But, Emerson, she seems to trust you. She might talk."

"And exactly what information do you want pumped from her, Mordechai?"

"A man. See if she talks about a new man, perhaps who went to work at the club before she left. Maybe as a bouncer. Maybe he had an accent, maybe he didn't."

"I'll ask."

"No, don't ask. You have hours in the car; let the conversation come around to it."

I still wasn't comfortable taking orders from Mordechai; I'd always been a little too independent. But Mordechai seemed to know more about what was going on than I did, so I nodded.

A few minutes later we went back inside, against the strict orders of Rebecca. She accepted us back into her fold like errant sheep, but I got the feeling that as soon as company (i.e., us) left, she had some shearing to do.

Remington had helped clean up (and hopefully gotten some cooking tips from Rebecca) and was ready to go by the time we came in. We thanked our hosts, kissed Rebecca on the cheek, and left feeling content.

That is, until I had to tell Remington I was spending all day Saturday with another dame.

She smiled sweetly.

"That's fine," she said. "I trust you. Just remember, I've never worn that shade of lipstick."

The underlying threat — death or maiming, I'm not sure which — was evidently all the objection she was going to raise.

I dropped her off at her apartment, then drove to my own. Tacked to my door I found a response to my notice of vacating the premises — a gruff "Make sure it's as clean as it was when you moved in or you won't get your deposit back" from Mr. Ewen and a "Don't mind him, sweetie. We'll miss you. Call us if you need to borrow our truck to move your things" from Mrs. Ewen.

I went in and called Sarah's cellular phone.

"Yes?" she answered almost immediately.

"It's Emerson. Let Maggie know I need an extra driver for my trip to Dallas tomorrow. I'll be by at about 7:30 A.M., and I hope she's not allergic to dogs."

"She knows, and she'll be ready."

Sarah hung up without any fanfare — maybe before I could say anything more. Cellular phones are easily listened in on — my police scanner could pick them up from time to time.

I set the alarm and hit the sack.

Then I suddenly wondered how Sarah was able to find out who my landlord was so quickly — she'd had everything squared with him within minutes after the shooting. Well, I'd given her and Mordechai the address; with the right connections in the tax office, she could have called and gotten the owner's name. Then she could have just used a phone book. I'm sure with her sweet voice and persuasive manner — but more likely with cash — she was able to convince Mr. Olsen that I'd need the place a little sooner than expected.

That connection in the tax office is what kept me awake for a few minutes. Sarah Tate hadn't been around town long; chances are she arrived just about the same time as Margaret. It had taken me months to develop sources within that office (those sources are quite valuable when you want to make sure a political candidate doesn't owe any back taxes). There was a pretty good chance that Sarah hadn't gone through the tax office at all; if the Mossad was working on something in this tiny burg in southeast Texas, maybe it was working with the Feds, who would have easy access to the information. That was some comfort.

As I dropped off to sleep I was still wondering what link an Irish exotic dancer could have with the Mossad.

And it all came back to the money and cocaine.

When the alarm went off, I showered and grabbed a couple of bagels. Bagels travel well (better than most children, I'm told). I filled a thermos with coffee and headed out. I arrived at my new house (one I apparently now officially rented but had yet to sleep in) and found that Sarah and Maggie hadn't spent the day before just sitting around. The place now had nice curtains, blinds, and even a little more furniture.

Sarah let me in, and I looked in wonder at what was becoming a quite livable home.

"Any requests?" Maggie asked.

"Yeah," I said. "That smaller bedroom will be a study. I've always wanted a nice mannish study. You know the kind? Paintings of ducks and sailboats, lots of dark wood, an oriental rug, et cetera. I have the paintings and all; I just wouldn't know how to set it all up right."

"Leave it to us," Sarah said. "I know just what you mean. How about forest-green wallpaper? It's the latest."

I considered it. "I'll take your word on it. Yeah, that sounds good. I'll leave some money for the materials."

"I just love doing this to other people's houses," Sarah said. "I'd never do it to my own, of course. I change my mind too much. I'd be painting rooms a new color every weekend."

Maggie went into a bedroom to get her purse. She came out and declared she was ready.

In the time I'd known Maggie, I was starting to see a change. She was wearing another T-shirt I knew was Remington's, and she was looking less and less like a mysterious, dangerous blonde. Instead, she was starting to look like a tired, worried young woman who just needed a little help and a little hope.

Help I could give. Hope comes from somewhere else.

"Let's go," she said. "I want to meet this dog. I love dogs."

"He's a charmer, all right," I said.

Before we got to the door, Sarah stopped us.

"Take my Jeep," she said. "It's got a full tank of gas, and I don't trust that land yacht of yours."

"I think I'm insulted," I said. "That pile of junk is a very respectable pile of junk."

"We can't afford the exposure of you two being stranded on the side of a road between here and Dallas," she said.

"I'll swallow my pride and accept your offer," I said. "Mainly because your Jeep probably has a more dependable air conditioner. Can't have Maggie sweating all over my poor dog."

I gave my keys to Sarah.

"If you need to go anywhere, it's not a complicated car," I said. "Just don't rely too heavily on the parking brake — try not to stop on hills, and don't worry if it starts to sound like a dying walrus. That's just the engine, nothing important."

"I'll be just fine," she said. "Mordechai will be out later, and I'm sure he'll bring me anything I'll need."

Maggie followed me out the door. I got the thermos and the bagels from my car and took them to the Jeep. Maggie was already situating herself in the passenger's seat when I got in on the other side.

"I sure appreciate this help," I said. "It's going to be a long drive."

Maggie just smiled at me. She started tilting her seat back.

"Are you going to psychoanalyze me too?" she asked.

"What?"

"Come on — Sarah is a sweet woman, but she's been at it for days. I think she's a cop of some kind; she keeps asking me about my old boss."

I pulled onto the farm-to-market road and headed towards Interstate 45, the highway leading through Houston and up to Dallas.

"She's not a cop," I said. "I'm not sure what she is, but she's on our side. And from what I know of this Garrett Maxwell, your old boss, he isn't."

"Is he trying to kill me?"

"I don't know. I don't know who's doing that."

"I know it's not you."

I smiled. "You must put a lot of stock into what Sally Nix told you. By the way, what did she tell you?"

"That you're a good man."

"Wrong. I've got all kinds of nasty habits. I'm generally not worth the time of day."

"You're my idea of a good man."

She lifted her hands to her face, a little embarrassed.

"I'm sorry," she said. "I don't want you to think I'm coming on to you. I'm not. I think the world of A. C. I think she's a lucky girl, that's all. With someone like you . . ."

"With someone like me what?"

"A woman would feel worth something."

"Well, thanks," I said. "But we've got to get something out of the way here. I was thinking about this last night. Sally sent you to me for help."

"Right, but not as much help as you've given me. I don't think this was part of the deal."

"Not part of Sally's deal, at least. But don't worry about it. By the way, did you ever talk to Trish?"

"Trish? Yeah, I called. I left a message at the bar. Sarah didn't want me to give out the cellular phone number, so I just said I'd call back in a couple of days."

"So Trish really is a friend of yours?"

"I guess so. I was closer to her than any of the other girls. She's the only one I miss. She cried when I cleaned out my locker."

"What about your boyfriend? Do you miss him?"

Maggie didn't respond for a moment. Finally she said softly, "I don't owe him anything, he doesn't owe me anything. That's that."

"OK. Now, Maggie my dear, tell me about your future."

She was silent.

"You haven't thought much about that in the past week, have you? I can understand that. In a situation like yours, you get pretty thankful just to make it through another day."

"I've been living like that for a long time now."

"What do you mean?"

"Day to day — just trying to make it through another one, and dreading the next."

"There's more, you know," I said. "You hoped for a future, didn't you? When you asked Sally to help you get out of — well, what you were doing?"

"I hoped for too much."

"I don't think so. I think you stopped short."

"Stopped short of what?"

"Any real future. Do you really think you can do it by yourself? Honestly?"

"No."

Her mouth — without lipstick this morning — was tight. She wasn't smiling. But she was listening.

"I agree. I couldn't either. Believe me, I was as bad off as you."

"What happened?"

"Martin Paige, a very good man, gave me hope — or at least showed me where to find it."

"Is this where religion comes in?"

I laughed. "Nope. I'm not so great at religion. In fact, I'm pretty bad at it. Ask me someday about the cigars. But this is different. Religion is one thing; this is another. Religion is what we try to do for God — which can't add up to much in the grand scheme of things. Christianity isn't like that. It's all about what God has done for us."

"I'm not the type, Emerson."

"Neither was I."

I let it go for a while, driving along the back roads to the interstate. But within five minutes Maggie spoke up again.

"What do you mean, what God has done for us?"

"He took care of it," I said. Then, remembering Martin's lesson on Wednesday, I added, "Him for us. Simple as that."

"It doesn't sound simple."

"It was simple enough when I needed it," I said. "I was out of work, out of drugs, and just about out of time when Martin told me about it. After that things seemed to clear up. Not instantly, but slowly and surely."

"When was this?"

"A few years ago. I wasn't an overnight success. I wasn't even an overnight Christian. It took a few weeks for the truth to sink in. But when I went into it, I went in knowing all the facts."

"What are you asking for?"

"I'm not asking for anything. I'm just offering. If you're interested I can tell you a little more about it. There's this guy, Jesus, you see . . ."

She laughed a little. "Yeah, I think I've heard about Him. Nice guy, wore robes a lot, and liked kids?"

"That's it."

"Well, go on. Like you said, it's going to be a long drive. I might as well listen. That can't hurt me, right?"

And then something slipped into sync. Suddenly we were talking, and I could feel the day brighten, and the desperate situations seemed almost petty. I pulled a small New Testament/Psalms from my pocket (OK, I'd gone in armed for this), and we started just reading through the first part of the Gospel of John.

"I've never really heard it like this," Maggie said. "It seems so different. Maybe they read a different version in church."

"Maybe," I said. "The version doesn't really matter all that much. It's the information involved."

We talked for a while about what she believed — or at least what she thought she believed.

"I don't know," she said. "Maybe I've just been ignoring this for so long I've gotten a little numb. For years I didn't feel bad about what I'd been doing — dancing. I didn't think I was hurting anyone."

"But something made you seek out Sally and eventually me," I said. "What was that? Guilt?"

"Maybe. Or depression."

"They feel a lot alike, and God uses both."

"Are you saying God caused that?"

"Sometimes," I said, "He pushes people a little bit. Most of the time we need it."

"So what do you have to do?"

"There's not much to it," I said. "Trust. Just like you decided to trust me."

We pulled onto the interstate, and I set the Jeep's cruise control. I leaned back, and Maggie poured some coffee into the cup on the thermos.

"Here," she said, handing me the cup. "Now, what's the catch?"

"Catch?"

"What else do I have to do?"

"Well, nothing really. I mean, you don't have to do anything. Salvation is free. But you'll start finding that you want to do more. I find myself doing stuff I didn't even know I wanted to do. Did you know I teach a junior high Sunday school class?"

"I can believe that."

"I wouldn't have. But it's been working out fine, and I really like it now. Remington helps. You know, she hasn't been at this Christianity stuff long. If you have any questions going in, you might want to talk to her some."

"I think I can talk to you. Is this how you usually do it?"

"Do what?"

"Talk about God — telling other people. So informally."

"Yeah, I guess. I'm not big on formality."

"Did you tell Remington? Oh, see, *I'm* doing it now. You call her by her last name. I mean A. C. Did you tell her?"

"Martin and his wife helped."

"How did she handle it?"

"Pretty well, I imagine. She's helping me teach that Sunday school class."

By the time we hit Corsicanna, about an hour south of Dallas, we'd gotten through most of her questions. I prefer it when someone has questions; I feel more honest about the whole thing. It tells me they know what they're getting into. I didn't press Maggie; when she was ready for more, the Holy Spirit would do the pushing.

11

do have some questions for you," I said as we continued driving north. "About your old job."

"Go ahead."

"Was Garrett Maxwell dealing?"

"These are the same questions Sarah was asking. I told her I wasn't sure; I tried to not pay attention."

"But was he?"

"Yes."

"How was it distributed?"

"Mostly through the dancers. The girls live on tips, and on a slow night that's not enough. It seems like big money at first, but it doesn't beat a steady paycheck. So sometimes when a girl was having a bad night, Maxwell would slip her an extra $50 to take a little package from one customer and give it to another; or sometimes it would be a little larger package she'd drop off at an address on her way home — at about 3:00 in the morning."

"Did you ever do this?"

"Sure."

"How big was his operation?"

"Was? It's still the second-biggest in Corpus."

"Second biggest?"

"There's a gang there. They think of themselves as part of some Los Angeles gang, but I don't think any of them have ever been out of the state. It's a bunch of kids, mostly. A twenty-two-year-old is the leader. They all drive metallic blue cars — Camaros, Corvettes, and the leader has a metallic blue BMW."

"And the kids distribute for him?"

"Yeah, twelve-year-olds and younger. They don't get prosecuted like adults or older kids do, so the gang members they look up to ask them to do it. It's kind of sad. But who am I to say anything? Look at what I was doing."

"Are there clearly defined territories?"

"Pretty much," she said after a moment. "The Crips have the inner city and around the port, and Maxwell keeps the rest of the county supplied."

"Does Maxwell want more?"

"Sure. Wouldn't you? So he's brought in some people."

Now we were getting somewhere. Maybe this is what Mordechai was looking for.

"What do you mean?" I asked.

"You know, some pros, I guess. Anyway, he calls them his lieutenants. And another man is training them. My old boyfriend was going to be a lieutenant, but the foreigner wouldn't take him. Said he was too arrogant."

Brian hadn't struck me as arrogant, but I filed that away for future reference.

"The guy who's training them is a foreigner?"

"Yeah. But he's kind of cute. Real dark, kind of like David. Talks like him, too. Maybe they're from the same country. Mean as a snake, though. I saw him hurt a girl once, just because she stopped to talk to him when she still had one of those packages in her purse. It's weird though — he was always nice to me."

Things were starting to add up. But there were still some things I needed to know; a trip to Corpus Christi was definitely on Sunday's agenda.

We got to my parents' house in east Dallas by 1 P.M. My dad was at work, but my mother was there to give us a quick lunch before we took Airborne and headed south again. I'd called her the night before to warn her we'd be by; she was a little disappointed we couldn't stay longer. So was I.

But Airborne was glad to see me. He'd grown a little thicker; he easily weighed ninety pounds by now. He'd burn off those extra calories at the farmhouse, I told my mom.

She asked discreetly about Remington, and I told her everything was fine and that Maggie was just a friend. Mom had met Remington at Easter when we went up for a long weekend.

Airborne hopped into the backseat of the Jeep and lay down for the ride. I'd forgotten how much he liked to ride in cars.

"What a cutie!" Maggie said as we pulled out of my parents' driveway. "He's so sweet — look at that face."

She reached around to pet him; he accepted it gracefully. He usually did.

My parents' home was about fifteen minutes from Interstate 45, so within half an hour we were leaving the Dallas skyline behind us. We stopped for gas at Ennis, and Maggie volunteered to drive for a while. I sat in back to spend some quality time with Airborne. I hugged his thick neck and scratched behind his ears. Doggie bliss.

"Did you miss me, you big ugly dog?"

"Don't talk to him like that. You'll hurt his feelings."

"I meant it in the nicest way possible. You should see what he says about me when I kick him off the bed at night."

"He's such a sweet dog," she said. "All we ever had were poodles — small, fluffy dogs that were awfully temperamental."

"Yeah, they get kind of wound up. You can't blame them though. It's their owners' fault. If someone put little bows in my hair like that, I'd be neurotic too."

"How long have you had him?"

"About three years, I guess."

I leaned back and relaxed for a while. There's something soothing about having a dog almost as big as you lounging at your side.

Near Madisonville we stopped and let Airborne explore a rest station's trees for a few moments and gave him some water. A few minutes later he was ready to resume his nap in the back-seat.

I took the wheel for the remainder of the trip. As we started getting nearer Houston, I could feel Maggie starting to tense up. We'd be talking about her family or mine, her high school prom or my freshman year at college, and she'd lose a train of thought.

"What's up?" I asked gently.

"It's been such a nice day," she said. "And now we have to go back. Someone wants me dead. Sometimes at night that thought doesn't bother me. I think maybe it would be easier. But now, I don't think so."

"Yeah, dead could be bad," I agreed. I paused for a moment. "Maggie, I don't mean to be harsh here, but let's face facts — you've been dead a long time now . . . deep down. I think you know what I mean."

She didn't say anything.

"Look," I said, "think it over. Like I said, I can't offer you much hope by myself. But there are a lot of people who can show you where to find it."

We drove on without speaking for another hour. Pretty soon we'd driven through the tangle of downtown Houston, down the highway leading toward my adopted hometown, and after a while we were nearing the farmhouse on that quiet farm-to-market road.

"Will you take me with you tomorrow?" she asked.

"Where?"

"To church. I might as well take a look. It's been so long since I've seen the inside of one."

"Sure. I'll pick you up at 9 A.M."

"I'm going to miss this smelly dog of yours," she said. "Bring him over sometime."

"Wait a minute," I said. "He's staying with you. I can't keep him at my apartment. But don't let him be Mr. Hoggy and steal all the covers. He'll do it, you know."

Maggie seemed delighted. She reached back and started scratching Airborne behind his ears again.

It was nearly 7:30 P.M. when we pulled into the driveway of the farmhouse; my car was still in the driveway, and David's Toyota was there too.

Airborne emerged from the Jeep to explore Doggie Paradise. We took him around to the fenced-in backyard and let him explore for a while. He was sniffing every tree, every rabbit hole, and everything else in the huge yard. He looked a little longingly at the fields that surrounded the yard and sniffed curiously at the air when he saw the eight or ten cows about a hundred yards off.

Maggie and I went in and found Sarah and David talking quietly. David grinned and without a word went out the back door to see Airborne. He loved the dog almost as much as I did; Rebecca never let him have a puppy either. He made up for lost time by spoiling Airborne during the one trip he and I took to Dallas. He went through half a box of doggie treats before I convinced him that Airborne wasn't picky — the dog would pay attention to him whether he bribed him with food or not.

Sarah gave Maggie and me a quick status report; nothing new had been blown up or shot through. Mordechai had boarded up his store's windows and, since he refused to work on a Saturday, planned to have some new glass installed on Monday.

Maggie and I took turns washing off the trail dust from the road trip. When I emerged, feeling almost human again, Sarah was in the kitchen, fixing what promised to be a wonderful dinner.

"I hope you didn't stop and eat on the way home," she said. "I'm fixing chicken. Mordechai will be over soon. He'll wait until sundown to drive here. Do you want to invite Remington? You can call her from my phone, but don't give directions."

"She knows the way," I said. "She'll love what you guys have done with the place so far."

"You haven't been in your study yet," Sarah said, turning and smiling at me. "David isn't only a wonderful photographer — he's also not bad with wallpaper."

I walked past the couch — and suddenly noticed a new rug and coffee table in front of it. On second glance, neither were new, but they were nice. I went down the hallway and into the bedroom on the left; the wallpaper was gorgeous, but it stopped before it reached the floor. David appeared at the door and said we would put up wood paneling, about three feet high, all the way around the room. The windowsill would be stripped and stained to match the paneling. The effect would be elegant, we agreed; it definitely would be a man's study. David had been busy, and it would likely take us two or three more weekends to finish the job. I wondered if I had enough money to foot the bill for this remodeling effort.

I went back to the kitchen and hugged Sarah.

"It's going to be beautiful," I said. "Now, how much do I owe you, you pushy old broad?"

"You'll get a bill," she said. "We're not through yet. I'm not quite sure what to do about the living room."

"I'll trust you on this."

David was behind me; I could tell because he smelled a little bit like a big dog. He didn't seem to mind, so I didn't object either. He entered the kitchen and filled a glass with water from the tap.

Then it hit me — I didn't have any glasses at the farmhouse; everything I owned was still at my apartment. I checked a couple of cabinets.

"Sarah, where did all of this come from?" I asked concerning the plates, glasses, and silverware. "You've already moved in. Where am I going to put all of my junk?"

"So many questions, Emerson. Don't worry. If your taste in china is as refined as your taste in furniture, from what David tells me hopefully it will all break in transit."

"That guy had the nerve to insult my furniture?"

"Not all of it, just the key pieces. Like that couch of yours. Is it really orange and green? A big floral print?"

"Those were very popular colors at one time."

Sarah looked a little concerned. "Emerson, that was thirty-five years ago. Are you telling me your couch is older than you are?"

"No. The couch is probably only about twenty-five years old. I'm twenty-eight. So there."

"Well, I guess you made your point," she quipped with a smile. "A. C. Remington has her work cut out for her, doesn't she?"

"I think I resent that. I'm a well-behaved young man. I'm even housebroken."

"Do you realize how lucky you are?"

"What do you mean?"

"How many girls would allow their boyfriends — their fiancés, if we're going to be realistic about this — to not only smoke nasty cigars with his buddies, but also to spend an entire day alone with a former exotic dancer, driving all over the state?"

I grinned. "OK, maybe I do get away with a lot. But I've given up the cigars — almost anyway."

"Call the poor girl and invite her over. We'll eat at about 8:30."

I dialed her number.

"Hello?"

"Hey, Remington. We're back, with said dog. He's been asking about you. Listen, Sarah's fixing some chicken, and Mordechai is coming over. David's already here. Why don't you come over too?"

"Fine. The new place?"

"Yeah."

"Great. See you soon."

I hung up and told Sarah to make David set another place at the table.

David was lying on the couch reading a *Time* magazine.

"I heard that," he said. "What am I, a servant around here? I do your wallpaper, I set the table. What next, I do the dishes?"

"Fine idea, David. You're a true friend."

He threw the magazine at me.

"So are we going to plan for tomorrow?" he asked.

"I guess we'd better. All we know is the name of the club. I guess Maggie could give us directions."

"I've got you a map, highlighted," Sarah said.

She handed us a satchel; it had a map, some cash, and another compact cellular telephone.

"Use the phone only when you have to," she said. "And never give out details. Police scanners, the kind anyone can buy at Radio Shack, can pick these up."

I knew that. A business card was also in the bottom of the leather pouch.

"The number on the card is a close friend," she said, with emphasis on the word "friend." "If you get in trouble, call him. Tell him Sarah sent you."

The card was that of a tax accountant. What would he do — fend off IRS agents? But I accepted it; you never could have convinced me before that this big-haired, would-be interior designer could be a bodyguard, or maybe even a spy. So what did I know about tax accountants?

Maggie came out of the bedroom. Sarah asked her to sit at the kitchen table.

"Maggie, I need you to draw the boys a map of the inside of Club Paradise. All doors, all windows, every room."

"It has two floors, you know," she said.

"I thought it did," Sarah said. "But I never got in. I couldn't tell from the outside if it was two stories or just a big warehouse-type ceiling."

Maggie took the pencil and graph paper Sarah gave her and began drawing. On a second sheet she drew another, smaller floor plan.

Sarah called David and me over to the table. We sat at the two remaining chairs and looked at the drawings.

"Now, Maggie, tell us where the bouncers are on a typical Sunday night."

"Well, Sunday is a slow night, usually. It's mainly just men who dread going back to work in the morning, so they go out just so they can say they had a wild weekend. Only two bouncers work on Sunday nights. But that's also when Mr. Maxwell does the books from the weekend. He'll be there."

"Where will the bouncers stand?" Sarah asked.

"One will be by the door, to keep 'undesirables' out — like men who are already drunk or especially rowdy — and to watch to make sure no one drunk — or at least too drunk — leaves without the club offering to get them a cab."

"That's a liability thing," I said. "Bars are getting sued left and right for letting drunks out onto the street. Most think if they just offer someone a cab, they're doing their job."

"Yeah, that's what Mr. Maxwell kept talking about during staff meetings. Oh, and the doorman will be looking for cops. He has some way of signaling the owner, the bartender, the DJ, and the other bouncer that cops or people who look like narcs are coming in. Then the DJ has a special thing he says, and it lets all the girls who are carrying for Maxwell know to dispose of the drugs."

"What's the signal?" I asked.

"He'll say, 'All right, all right, we're partying down tonight.' It sounds like harmless DJ chatter, but the girls all know what it means."

"And where's the other bouncer?" Sarah asked.

"He'll be watching the floor. Sometimes a state guy can slip in undercover — the state Alcoholic Beverage Commission. They're the ones who arrest girls for going too far, like coming within twelve inches of a customer. The charge is public lewdness. So the second guy will be watching the girls to make sure they stay on just this side of the line — you know what I mean?"

I nodded.

"And watch the waitresses," Maggie added. "If they see anything strange, they'll whisper in the bartender's ear, and he'll alert everyone else. There will be three or four waitresses on a Sunday night."

"Where's the staircase?" I asked, pointing to the drawing of the bottom floor.

"Oh, it's behind the bar. Customers can't get to it except by going through the bar and past the bartender."

"And how dark will it be?" I asked.

"The corners and sides will be dark, and the stage with the dancers — they take turns on it — will be so bright that it makes everything else seem even darker."

"What do the dancers do when they're not dancing?" David asked.

"They mill around," Maggie said. "Here's the deal: a dancer isn't paid anything. Nothing at all by the club. She's considered contract labor. She lives solely on tips, and she has to share those with the bartender and the waitresses. So anyway, she shows up, gets a spot in the lineup, and when the DJ calls her name, she'll take the stage. Guys will tip her some then, but that's really only to get the dancer's attention. A guy that wants to see her more will tip her a little more; if he tips her a five dollar bill, she'll know to go sit with him when she's through. Then the girl really starts making money. First, he'll offer her a drink. She's not allowed to ask, but she doesn't ever have to. She'll order an expensive drink, and the bartender will go real light on the alcohol since dancers can't be drunk — that's against the law too. But she gets a little money for every drink a guy buys her. The waitress keeps tabs on it. And then, after talking to the guy for a while and sounding really interested in him, he'll start getting the feeling that she likes him. But all she sees are dollar signs. The real money comes from the table dance. That's when a dancer will do her act for the guy, all by himself — sort of a private show. That's what all the dark corners are for. She still can't get too close to him, but that's where the rules are bent the most. Anyway, that's where the real money is made. The going rate for a table dance is only about $25, but it can add up. On a good night you can do five or six — sometimes more."

"What about the dancers? What's their loyalty to the bar owner, this Maxwell guy?" I asked.

"Well, what do you mean? If you mean, will they stand between him and a bullet, no. They wouldn't even stand between him and a cop. If they knew how much he was setting them up by paying them to deliver his drugs —"

Sarah's eyes narrowed. Maggie had played dumb about this with her before.

"Go on," I said.

"Well, if there's trouble, don't expect the girls to do anything but disappear. There are always other clubs. Most of these girls work at different ones on different nights of the week."

Maggie paused.

"And there's one more wild card — there's a foreign guy Maxwell has hired. He might be in there, he might not. If he is, he'll be hard to spot. He doesn't sit anywhere near a light."

"I don't think you'll have to worry about him," Sarah said. "Just concentrate on the owner. He'll probably have a gun up in that office."

"I think that's enough for us," I said. "Sarah, if you have any other questions for Maggie, I'm sure she'll be more cooperative about answering them."

I looked at Maggie, who was staring down at the table. "Maggie, I trust her. I think you can too. If she wasn't one of the good guys, she wouldn't have bought new plates for the farmhouse. Have you ever known an evil villain to buy plates for someone else?"

Maggie smiled. David and I got up and left the two women in the kitchen. David wanted to go back outside and see how Airborne was adjusting.

He was adjusting quite nicely, thank you — he was asleep on the porch by the back door, waiting for me to let him in.

"OK, guy," I told him. "But be nice to everyone. Don't eat anyone's shoes, and don't hog anyone's covers."

He looked agreeable to those conditions, so I let him in. The back door led through the kitchen and into the living room. He ambled in, past the stove (he paused to sniff up at it and confirm that food was being cooked) and straight over to the couch. Without missing a step he climbed up onto the couch as if he owned the place.

"Wait 'til Remington gets here," I told him. "She gets the final say on whether you and I are indoor dogs or outdoor dogs — and what furniture we have access to."

As if on cue, Remington's Volvo drove up to the old farmhouse. She'd helped me pick out the house, and she even convinced the landlord to lower the rent a little. She was one tough cookie. I didn't want to see Airborne's face when she banished him to the great outdoors.

She walked up carrying a grocery bag, and David opened the door for her.

"Hey, Dave," she said, "I just talked to Ruth. Why haven't you called her in three days? She's getting worried about you."

David shrugged. "I've been busy."

"Don't get too busy for her," Remington warned. "Think about what your mother would do to you if you lost Ruth."

"It's not me," he protested. "What time does she have for me?"

"Put your foot down then," Remington said. "You know how she is. She'll get so wrapped up in her dad's business, she'll put everything else aside. Don't let her do it. Call her up and tell her you love her and you're going out whether she likes it or not. And call her dad too. Shlomo will be on your side. He thinks she's working too much, and he knows how important you are to her."

As she walked to the kitchen, she commented on the work Maggie and Sarah had done on the house — the curtains, the new rug, and the coffee table.

Remington had her hair pulled back in a ponytail and was wearing jeans and a T-shirt. She must not have felt it was a formal occasion to be reunited with my dog. But she did drop the grocery bag on the kitchen table, then headed straight over to hug Airborne's neck. He wagged his tail appreciatively.

"You're not going to make him stay outside, are you?" Maggie asked, following Remington in from the kitchen. "He's so sweet. Look at that face."

"Oh, he can stay inside," Remington said. "I mean, it's not *my* house. I don't mind him being inside at all."

Remington may have put a little too much emphasis on the "my house" thing. At any rate I got that cold chill down my spine again. Still, Remington would be spending a lot of time here, and I wasn't going to force my dog upon her. I also had the feeling that she actually was growing quite fond of the mutt. I was glad of that; if she ever did end up being a permanent resident here or anywhere else with us, I wouldn't want there to be any conflicts.

Airborne resumed his natural posture (namely, sitting at the end of the couch, curled up on the last cushion with his head on the armrest) and just watched us. Shortly after the sun set, Mordechai arrived. He looked overjoyed to see us; then again, he always seemed overjoyed to see anyone who would laugh at his jokes.

"How was the trip to Dallas?" he asked.

"Nice," I said. "Long."

"You are tired, yes?"

"A little."

Sarah had dinner on the table by the time Mordechai had his coat off. Even in a Texas summer, Mordechai wore his suit coat. I was amazed.

There were six of us and only four chairs in the kitchen, so David and I brought two chairs in from the living room. We all squeezed around the small table. I took a look around at the ad-hoc household; it was a weird bunch to gather at one table. But the dinner conversation was relaxed. Mordechai somehow managed to eat twice as much as anyone else while at the same time talking twice as much as anyone else. Remington and Maggie got along just fine; those two hours of bonding — or whatever they call it these days — on the night Maggie's car was blown to bits must have cemented a friendship. I was glad to see it.

David, as usual, kept fairly quiet and concentrated on eating. Sarah prepared some coffee after the meal, and we all adjourned to the living room. Airborne, I'm saddened to report, was forced off his couch and made to sleep on the hardwood floor in front of it.

"And so, David and Emerson, tell me about tomorrow," Mordechai said, sipping some of Sarah's strong coffee; she'd added cardamom (a Middle Eastern spice) to it. I'd never had anything like it, but it wasn't bad.

"What's to tell?" David said. "We'll go down to Corpus Christi and go to a topless bar. We'll find out what we find out."

"That's the plan as I see it," I said. "Although, with Remington sitting here, I wouldn't have phrased it exactly in that manner. Dear, it's merely an investigation."

Remington smiled. "It had better stay that way, Dunn."

"Look, I didn't get myself into all of this," I said. "Sally Nix did."

"Sally is a good officer," Sarah said. "She knew what she was doing."

I paused. "You know Sally Nix?"

This time Sarah paused. "We've run into each other."

"That's all you're going to tell me?"

David sighed. "It's no use."

Mordechai looked at his nephew sternly. "You know what you need to know," he finally said.

"Fine," I said. "But somehow I think we're aiding your investigation more than you're aiding ours."

"What makes you think there are two different ones?" Sarah asked.

"Never mind."

Despite their stubborn refusal to reveal any information they thought we didn't need to know, the mood in the room was still relaxed and unstrained. I wasn't sure why we'd all been thrown together — in my prematurely rented farmhouse — but I figured good would come of it. I certainly hoped so at least.

Mordechai was just starting to order David into the kitchen to do the dishes (I would have helped) when we all stopped what we were doing and listened to a low, rumbling sound.

It was Airborne; he was growling.

"Down," came Mordechai's stern voice. At first I thought he was talking to Airborne, but then the sound of a shotgun enlightened me to the wisdom of his advice.

Five blasts came this time — two apparently aimed at each of the two living room windows that face the road, and a fifth that sounded like it peppered the door. It was a thick, solid wood door, so nothing made it through. The windows were a different story. The glass shredded the new curtains and rained down on us as we dove for the floor.

Remington had been sitting on the couch between David and me. Maggie had already been on the floor; she'd been on the rug petting Airborne. Mordechai and Sarah had been in the two chairs almost exactly facing the windows (the couch was right below one of them). David had grabbed Remington on his way down, but this time I was on my own. I landed face-first on the floor.

A second later there was silence. I looked around; everyone seemed fine.

"I knew this place wouldn't last," Sarah said. "We've done too much coming and going."

David was at the side of a window checking for any signs of movement in the yard or on the road. The house was set far enough back that for a shotgun blast to have been accurate, the assailant must have crept up pretty close. David shook his head, letting us know he saw nothing.

Mordechai was less interested in the windows than he was in

Airborne. Airborne looked calm now, as if the threat had gone away. Maybe it had.

"Emerson, open the front door."

"Oh, that sounds smart. Should I invite the guy in too? Offer him some coffee and a fresh clip of ammunition?"

"Shotguns don't have clips," Mordechai said, still watching Airborne. "Your dog is very protective but also very curious. If anyone is out there, he will go to the door. If not, he will stay."

"Yeah, I guess that's right."

I scooted over, avoiding as much glass as I could, and reached for the door. I turned the knob and flung the door open, away from me. I pulled back from it just in case the gunman had been reloading.

Airborne looked at the door with disinterest.

That satisfied Mordechai. He got up and closed the door.

12

O ur security has been violated," Mordechai said. "Maggie and Sarah, get your things. We'll leave as soon as we call the police and make a report."

I was afraid of that part. Calling the police wouldn't be a pleasant experience. At least Singer wasn't on duty.

A squad car came around. We filed a report, and the officer told me to expect a call from my favorite detective sergeant first thing Monday morning. Some shells were found behind a tree about ten yards from the front of the house; they were taken as evidence.

The patrol sergeant offered to leave a man at the house tonight. I thought it best to decline without mentioning the firepower we already had there.

When the cops left, about half an hour later, we sat at the kitchen table to discuss our options.

"My place has a full-time security guard at the gate," Remington said. "It's a small apartment, but Sarah and Maggie and I would be all right."

Mordechai nodded. "Good. That will do for now. But no more of this comings and this goings."

Maggie spoke up for the first time since dinner.

"But what about church?"

"Oy, oy, oy," Mordechai said. "OK . . . OK. But, David, you're to go too."

David looked a little amused; he'd never been to church before. He knew about my faith, but to him Jesus was just another offbeat rabbi — and there had been many, many offbeat rabbis through the centuries.

"Martin will love that," I said. "I hope you don't expect him to go in armed."

Mordechai laughed. "No. I know my nephew. He drives a tank, he runs over houses, he blows up buildings; still, he does not like guns."

"I don't think the pastor — our rabbi — would approve either," I said. I turned to David. "Maybe this is what you need, Dave, a little of that old-time religion," I said.

Remington snickered.

It was good to see Maggie so eager to go to church; maybe it was a sign she was sincere about wanting to change her lifestyle.

Mordechai said he'd send the glass man out to fix my windows on Monday just as soon his store was repaired. Sarah looked at the marks left by the shotgun blasts and declared them fixable.

The problem was what to do with Airborne. I figured I could sneak him into my apartment and if I was up early enough, I could sneak him back out. But what after that?

Then I had a thought — Martin's home had a fenced back-yard. I'd imposed on the poor pastor for food, lodging, guidance in spiritual and other matters, and I'd baby-sat (or is the word baby-sitted?) his kids, including Dangerous Sue, on occasions too numerous to count. I grabbed Sarah's cellular phone and dialed his number.

"Sure," he said when I explained my problem (and the five shotgun blasts preventing me from staying at my own new home). "As a matter of fact, why don't you both spend the night? He'll adjust a little better that way. You two can fight over the couch."

"Thanks, Martin," I said. "This almost makes up for giving me the junior high class."

"Well, Emerson, maybe you and I just share a habit of taking in strays."

"Maybe. I'll be by with toothbrush in hand in about half an hour."

"You know where the key is."

I hung up, and Mordechai was satisfied that everyone would be safe — for the night, at least.

"If we scatter, they don't know whom to follow, if they're interested in following at all," he said. "And after church, you boys leave for Corpus."

"Fine," I said.

We parted ways at the driveway. Mordechai left for David's house, Sarah and Margaret followed Remington to her place, and David followed me and Airborne out of the driveway.

I drove the ten minutes to my apartment and left the dog in the car while I vaulted up the stairs to grab a few things. I quickly found a Bible, a travel bag with an extra toothbrush, razor and other essentials, and the khaki slacks and white oxford shirt I planned to wear to church. I'd long ago given up on wearing ties to teach Sunday school. A tie automatically made the kids feel they were in school and should call me Mr. Dunn. I'd rather they relax a little and listen to what I had to say instead of considering it another lesson to wade through.

On the way over to Martin's house, I stopped off at the only all-night convenience store in town and bought a small bag of dog food. It would last a couple of days. Finally, with Airborne sprawled across most of the front seat (it was an old bench seat, the kind you don't see much anymore), we made it to Martin's. I walked up to the homey brick house with my dog in tow and found the spare key clinging to a magnet on the bottom of the porch swing. I let myself in. Martin was still awake, going over some notes at the kitchen table. He smiled as Airborne and I walked in.

"He doesn't have to stay inside," I said. "He'll be perfectly fine outside. I really appreciate this."

"It's up to you," Martin said. "But remember, we had a dog for years. And with you, Emerson, we know to not be surprised at whatever you bring home."

I grinned; he was probably making reference to various and sundry girls I'd dated in college. I made it a point to check out each one of them with Martin. A couple of them made him a little nervous, but you can't say I didn't warn him in advance about the one with the pierced nose. But that's a different story altogether.

Anyway, Airborne explored his new surroundings with little enthusiasm. I think the long drive and the excitement at the farmhouse had worn him out. I fixed him a bowl of water, put it right outside Martin's back door, and left Airborne to sleep just outside on the doormat.

"Martin, I think she's coming around," I said quietly, sitting across from him at the kitchen table. "I think you were right."

"About taking in the strays? I've always seemed to attract them," he said. "Maybe it's something you picked up from me. Sorry."

I smiled. "It's not a particularly bad habit, I guess. Not like making a habit of house cleaning or anything. It's kind of rewarding. On the trip up to Dallas we talked quite a bit. I think she's still stumbling on one point."

"What's that?"

"'Him for us' is the way you put it."

"Substitutionary atonement. That's the seminary phrase for it."

"Yeah, that. She's coming out of a situation where everything — the most basic parts of a relationship: affection, interest, physical contact — were strictly cash transactions. She doesn't quite seem ready to accept anything for free yet. Or at least she wasn't today. But you know me — I'm no high-pressure salesman.

Maybe you can do better tomorrow. She wants to come to church."

"I'll hit on that during my sermon," Martin said after a pause. "I can work it in. But, Emerson, I'm worried about something else. It might come as a surprise to you, but I find it a little disturbing when a friend of mine barely escapes two drive-by shootings. What's going on?"

I told him what I could. His eyes narrowed when I told him David and I were going to a topless bar on Sunday night. I also told him what I could about Sarah and Mordechai, the two unknown factors in all of this.

"I realize that's a little hard to believe — Israeli spies operating in a small town like this," I said. "But all the facts point to it. And Mordechai keeps giving orders, and I keep following them."

"What's the real purpose in going down to Corpus Christi, Emerson?"

I paused. No one — not me, not David, not even Mordechai — had put it into words yet.

"I think it's information gathering mostly," I said. "Something about the drug operation is linked to Maggie. But that's going to be David's job. I've got a different agenda."

"What's that?"

"Well, it's certainly not to step into the middle of a gang war. I've seen too many of them come and go. From my perspective, the only thing I expect we'll be able to salvage from all of this is a young woman named Margaret Sullivan. Someone is trying to kill her — or maybe just scare her into giving up the cocaine and the money she allegedly stole. But, Martin, she says she didn't take anything, and I believe her. Mordechai and Sarah can fight the other battles. I'm going to find out why this Garrett Maxwell thinks she stole his money and drugs, and I'm going to put his suspicions to rest."

Martin watched me for a moment. Something in his eyes told me that I'd come to the right place.

"It's not going to be easy," he said. "You're the reporter, you know more about crime than I do. But I know that look, Emerson. You're convinced she's clean and that you can save her."

"I wouldn't put it that way."

"Maybe you should. Go ahead with it, Emerson. But realize two things first. One, you can't do it alone. You might help save her skin, but that still leaves her soul. And second, the Bible doesn't say anywhere that Emerson Dunn is bulletproof. I know — I've read the whole Bible, even the maps."

I smiled. "But, Martin, if I were to, say, get large holes blown through me, can you think of a better reason? Wouldn't you do the same thing?"

He ignored the question. "There are a lot of people who would miss you, including one A. C. Remington."

I nodded. He looked up at me a little curiously.

"Emerson, exactly what do you plan to call that girl once you marry her?"

The worldwide conspiracy had widened; it had now even taken in Martin Paige, an influential pastor. My heart started beating a little faster.

"Martin, who said anything about marriage? You know, I still kind of miss Vicky — you remember, the girl with the pierced nose?"

13

had to wait my turn behind Martin, his wife Meg, his two daughters, and his son before I got a shot at the shower. I used the time to console an extremely disinterested Airborne, who hadn't been bothered in the least by spending the night outdoors.

"You've got to behave now," I said. "Don't whine and make them think I'm a bad father."

He looked up at me with puppy-dog eyes (I expected that, of course).

"Oh, I'll be back soon, and maybe after all this is over, we can live in peace in our farmhouse," I said. "No one will be around to make us take flea baths when we don't want to, and we can drink milk right from the carton. Except for you, I guess. Drinking milk from the carton might be a little hard for a dog, but you can try if you want."

Ricky came onto the porch, not bothered in the least by the fact that when he went to bed he only had to deal with a normal family, and when he awoke he had to deal with a normal family plus a "mature" adult who was talking to a dog in the backyard.

"Hey, Emerson," he said, "is this your dog?"

"Yeah," I said. "Do you remember him from Dallas?"

"He wasn't this big."

"Neither were you."

"Yeah. Is he going to stay with us?"

"Just for a night or so. Then I'll take him to the new house I'm moving into, the one out in the country. He would be out there now, but we had a little problem."

"What kind of problem?"

I examined the six-year-old, who was already tired of summer and ready to start first grade. The blond hair he'd had as a baby was darkening, and he was growing up to be a stout, sturdy kid. He enjoyed sailing with me, and since Remington had been so busy of late, I'd taken him out on Clear Lake at least every other week or so.

If a kid crews for you, you've gotta be honest with him.

"Someone came and added a little air conditioning to the new house."

"What?"

"They shot it up with a shotgun. There's a girl, a girl you'll meet at church, who is in a little trouble with some bad guys."

Ricky nodded, still not bothered in the least. "Did anyone get shot?"

"No."

"Can you get her out of trouble with the bad guys?"

"Maybe. I'm going to try."

Ricky, still standing, put his arm around my shoulder. A six-year-old was lending me some confidence.

"If you pray about it, I bet you can do it," he said. "In children's church we talk about getting in trouble. You can get into trouble, but you can get out. All you gotta do is be ready to take the consequences."

"The consequences," I said. What's a six-year-old doing walking around with a four-syllable word?

"Yeah. You know what those are?"

"Well, why don't you explain it to me?"

"It means that sometimes if you do something bad, something bad will happen. Jesus forgives you, but He doesn't always stop the bad things from happening."

Ricky's voice dropped to a bare whisper. "Like getting in trouble at school. If I get in trouble at school, Jesus will forgive me, but the teacher will still call my dad. Then I'll really get it."

I nodded, knowing full well the meaning of "I'll really get it."

"Thanks, Ricky. I think you've helped me out some. I think you're right. If this girl is in trouble, she'll have to accept the consequences. All I have to do is figure out if she really should be in trouble or not."

Ricky patted me on the shoulder, the camaraderie of fellow mariners.

I followed him back into the house; it was my turn in the shower. I made it quick and was ready within about ten minutes. I then helped Meg get eggs and sausage onto the plates and into the faces of three impatient kids. When I pushed her a little bit on the dog issue, she assured me she didn't mind a bit and even asked if I had a leash so she could take him with her on her evening walk.

"Sure," I said. "He'd love that."

We packed the kids into the cars (Ricky rode with me) and got to the church by 9:15. Remington and Maggie were already there, getting the classroom ready. I lingered outside for a few minutes until David arrived. He looked a little nervous until Martin came and put him at ease. David followed me into the classroom, where Remington and Maggie were arranging the chairs in a circle.

"What's the lesson for today?" Remington asked after she kissed me hello (she was starting to do that in public now).

"You're looking at him," I said, poking David in the ribs.

"What?" Remington and David asked in unison.

"Oh, come on, could I pass up an opportunity like this? We've got a guy here who was born and raised in the Holy Land. To these kids, the Bible is all about places and people in some other time, some other world. David is going to tell them about Israel and Jerusalem and Bethlehem and all those things."

David nodded. He was an easygoing guy, and I knew he was

used to dealing with kids (during the school year he taught Hebrew to twelve-year-olds getting ready for their bar mitzvahs at a synagogue in Houston).

"Yeah, I can do that," he said.

The kids started piling in, wondering about the fresh influx of adults. Dennis, one of my favorite (if more exasperating) students, knew David already. Dennis came into the newspaper office sometimes when he needed a little help in his reading and writing classes (they call them "language arts" classes now).

Maggie took a seat beside Remington in the circle, but Samantha, an outgoing eighth grader, had already set her sights on Maggie and was moving in to find out about this new woman she hadn't seen in church before.

After the bell sounded and the fifteen or so kids got quiet, I introduced David.

"Cool!" one kid said. "He's Israeli? Like on the news? Boy, they're tough."

"Is that like the children of Israel — in the Bible?" Samantha asked.

"Yeah," I said. "Same bunch."

Forget a lesson plan; the kids had enough questions to fill up three or four hours. A lot of the boys had questions about the Israeli military. David saw a trend and did what he could to bring the discussion back to where he knew I wanted it.

"In the army we have a lot of our ceremonies at the Wailing Wall in Jerusalem," he said. "Do any of you know what that is?"

He got a bunch of blank stares.

"Believe it or not, that wall is the last remaining wall of the Great Temple," he said.

Even Dennis looked a little skeptical.

"You mean the Temple in the Bible? But none of that's still around, is it?" he asked.

"Of course it is," David said. "You should see Jerusalem. You read about it in your Bibles, but it's also a real place. Help me out, Emerson."

"OK, guys, remember a few weeks ago when we talked about Jesus cleansing the Temple?" I asked.

"Yeah, He turned over all those tables because everyone was getting greedy and trying to make money off of God," Dennis said.

"Close enough. Well, the Wailing Wall is one wall of that Temple. David here was awarded a bunch of medals standing in front of the wall — probably on ground that Jesus walked on."

The class seemed to think about that one for a moment. But then, out of the blue, came the one question we weren't ready for.

"David, do you believe in Jesus?"

I gulped. Since we were all in a circle, I could see Remington's surprised face. The question had come from Samantha.

David sighed. "I am a Jew," he said. "You read about them in your Old Testament, and a little in your New Testament. So you know a little about Jews. But I don't know much about Jesus. I never really met a Christian before I met Emerson. Now sometimes I wonder. Not about whether I believe in Jesus, because even Jews believe that a rabbi named Jesus existed. But Emerson, and Martin, your preacher, say that Jesus was the Son of God. That is what I wonder about."

Samantha wasn't satisfied.

"What's the problem, then? Why not stop wondering and find out?"

"Sam, I really think —"

"No, I can handle this, Emerson," my friend said. "Samantha, remember the Nazis?"

"Yeah."

"Most of them considered themselves Christians. For many, many centuries other people who considered themselves Christians have been hard on Jews. We are blamed for killing Jesus. Many world leaders, like Hitler and some others before him, and some after him also, have wanted to kill all Jews. So you see, for us Christianity has meant trouble. It's a little hard to consider Jesus as someone good when so much bad has been done by people who say they love Him. Until I met Emerson — and Remington, and Martin — I didn't trust anyone who said he was a Christian."

David paused for a moment. "There's one part of Israel that's not in your Bible, but maybe it should be. There is a grove of trees planted in memory of Christians who helped Jews during the Holocaust, when Hitler was trying to kill us all."

I looked at my watch; mercifully, the hour was almost over. I wasn't sure if this had been a good or bad idea. Was it too confusing to the kids? I think Dennis answered that question for me a few minutes later, after the prayer and after the bell rang. He walked up to David as we were about to close up the room.

"Hey, Dave, stick around for church," he said. "The Christians here are more like the ones you guys planted trees for. At least that's what I think."

I think Dennis, and maybe the others, would do just fine with the information. I hoped David didn't mind being my "show and tell" for the morning.

14

The four of us — Remington, Maggie, David, and I — filed into the sanctuary of the small church as the organist began playing. David looked at the church decorations, pews, and pulpit with mild curiosity. There were two rows of pews with a wide aisle between them. We sat toward the back, close to the aisle. For David and Maggie's sake, we tried to remain inconspicuous.

David had met Martin — he'd even eaten at Martin's house once or twice with me — but he'd never heard Martin preach. Martin was off to the side of the pulpit, talking to a deacon, when he saw us come in. He came over a moment later.

"A. C., you look lovely," he said. She blushed a little, as she always did. "You must be Maggie. Emerson and A. C. speak quite highly of you."

And then he looked at David and grinned.

"Does your mother know you're here?" he asked.

David grinned back. "No."

David's mother, a Conservative Jew, probably wouldn't have approved of David going to church.

"I won't tell if you won't," Martin said. "And, Emerson, I got a good report out of your Sunday school class."

"Good," I said. "It was an experiment. I'm not sure yet if it worked."

"I'll back you on anything that will help the kids know that the Bible stories they read are about real places," Martin said. He looked over at Maggie. "You're in good hands here."

"Yeah," she said, looking him straight in the eyes. I think she was looking for something. She smiled at him warmly; maybe she'd found it.

Martin went to greet a few other people as a couple of deacons — and a couple parents of junior high kids — came over to us. Samantha's mom went straight to David and thanked him for being "guest speaker" for my class — Samantha had told her about it right away. She also asked David if he would mind speaking at the ladies' Bible study some Thursday night. David said, "Sure," a little flattered.

Five or six parents came by and made a comment or two; none were negative. Apparently we hadn't shaken anyone's faith; we just made them think about it a little differently.

In fact, having David along might have taken a little pressure off Maggie. People still greeted her, but no one asked too many questions.

The service started with the normal music, prayers, and sitting and standing for no apparent reason. Neither David nor Maggie knew the songs, but no one seemed to mind.

Martin's sermon was indeed almost completely aimed at Maggie. At least, that's obviously how Maggie felt. I don't know if it was good timing or if Martin had pulled his intended sermon and substituted the one from the fourth chapter of John. Maggie and I had gone over the story of the Samaritan woman at the well in the car on the way to and from Dallas, but I hadn't pushed it. The woman, amazed that a religious Jew such as Jesus would even condescend to speak to her, believed in Him when He not only pointed out her sins (she'd had five husbands, plus another man around who wasn't her husband), but also when Christ revealed His compassion.

"Christ asked nothing of her," Martin said. "He offered her the living water — eternal life, a well of hope — without asking anything in return. Her life changed, as we see later on in the chapter, and God used her to bring many to Him. But up front there was no price."

I wasn't sure how Maggie was taking it. Martin wasn't hammering on anyone, but he also wasn't glossing over the need the woman at the well — and everyone else — has.

When the sermon started winding down, I looked over at Maggie. She was whispering to Remington.

Martin closed his sermon as he often did: "It's not a difficult decision. You can make it right where you sit."

Martin asked that we all bow our heads. We did so, but I felt Maggie's hand on my arm. A short squeeze. I wasn't sure what it meant, but I had high hopes.

The music continued playing as Maggie and Remington whispered softly to each other. When the service ended, we filed out of the pew. Remington caught my hand and leaned to whisper in my ear.

"She's a little nervous, but then I was too," Remington said. "I think she's going to be OK."

Remington had let Christ into her life a few months earlier, and now it appeared Maggie had made the same wise decision.

During the brief milling-about period after the service, Meg (Martin's wife) invited all four of us over for lunch. It was with exceeding regret that we declined. Meg said Ricky had promised to take good care of Airborne, so David and I followed Maggie and Remington back to Remington's apartment.

When we arrived, Sarah was on the phone — a brand-new phone on the wall, not the one from her purse. Apparently the telephone company had hooked it up over the weekend. Sarah had a steno pad full of notes, and it looked like she'd been on the phone all morning.

"Just doing a little work," she said. "Boys, are you ready for your trip?"

"I guess so," I said.

"Well, take the Jeep again. Here are the keys. I think it's about time for the girls to go shopping. The malls are open all after-noon."

I kissed Remington good-bye.

"Be careful," she said. "And don't come back with any lipstick anywhere on your person."

"Trust me," I said.

"Emerson, you two have to handle this delicately," Sarah said. "When Sally Nix left abruptly, right at the same time Maggie did, the task force thought it had lost six months of work. But so far there's no indication that Maxwell suspects anything. They're going to try to salvage the sting operation; don't do anything that might compromise it. Just show up, get a little information if you can, and leave."

"Sarah, now you're sounding like a cop," I said. "Will I ever get to find out what you really are?"

"Sure, sweetie," she said. "I already told you — I'm your guardian angel."

"What kind of angel packs an automatic pistol?"

"A smart one. Now you two hit the road. We have shopping to do."

Sarah handed David the leather pouch with the map, the cash, and the all-important tax accountant's phone number. She also handed us a small ice chest with sandwiches and soft drinks. She was probably a little more maternal than your average spy, but we appreciated the food. I followed David out the door and down to Sarah's Jeep.

"I'll drive first," he said.

"Fine."

I got in on the passenger's side once David had unlocked the door.

"By the way, Dave, thanks for the compliment," I said. "In Sunday school."

He nodded.

Within a few minutes we were on a highway headed toward Corpus Christi, about a four-hour drive away.

David wasn't in a talkative mood; he seemed a little apprehensive.

"OK, Dave, come clean. We've been ordered to get information, but no one has told me what information to get. That means they must have told you. Spill it."

He grimaced and said nothing.

"I won't ask if it means you have to disobey any orders, but I sure would like to know what we're looking for."

He paused. "He's in the Galveston area somewhere."

"Who?"

"The person that Sarah and Mordechai are looking for. The one who's trying to kill Maggie, I guess. We're supposed to find out where. That's all I know. We must look for the name of a hotel, a telephone number, even telephone messages. But that's all I can tell you."

"That means getting into the owner's office."

"Yeah, I know."

"We'll figure out a way."

"I've got some ideas."

"That scares me, Dave. Maybe Ruth is right in not letting you think for yourself too much. It gets you and others in trouble."

He grinned and again said nothing.

By 6 P.M. we were in Nueces County. The bar was located off a semi-major highway, just outside the Corpus Christi city limits.

I shouldn't have been concerned about not finding the place. It was a big green-and-yellow building, painted to catch the attention of motorists speeding by, with a neon sign proclaiming, CLUB PARADISE. The driveway and parking lot were gravel; about five cars were parked at the side of the building, and about ten or twelve were parked in a loose line out in front. It was an interesting array of vehicles. We parked next to a BMW, but on the other side of us an old pickup threatened to spread its rust like a disease to Sarah's new-looking Jeep. We locked the doors and went inside.

If I hadn't been wearing sunglasses outside, I'd have been

blind walking in. Despite the full fury of the afternoon Texas sun, the bar was dark — very dark. I could see a few customers, but the place was far from packed. A man in a sharp blue blazer and white pants — and even a tie — greeted us as we walked in.

"Good evening, gentlemen," he said in a businesslike tone. He was a big guy, with a big chest and meaty arms that the tight blazer wasn't trying to hide. He was obviously a well-mannered bouncer.

"Hi," I said. "Need to see our IDs?"

"Please."

He glanced at our licenses and stepped aside to let us in; apparently there was no cover charge on a Sunday night. They were probably happy for any business they could get.

The place was just as Maggie had described it. The bar was to our left and the stage to our right. A dancer was in the preliminary part of her routine — that is to say, she still had clothes on — but David and I weren't interested in her. We were more interested in sighting that other bouncer. I followed David to a table in a dim corner. A waitress came by and asked us what we'd like.

Nothing would make them more suspicious than ordering a Coke in a bar, I realized. I hoped Martin would understand and ordered two overpriced drinks.

A few moments later another girl walked by. She carried a tray of cigarettes and cigars, just like they did in the 1940s. I hadn't ever seen a cigarette girl in real life. David grinned and bought us two cigars.

"The cigars will allow us to linger here longer without drinking," he said. "I can't afford to drink. I can't afford to lose my edge."

I nodded. "I'm planning to abstain too. But the drinks sitting on the table will make us blend in a little better. I feel a little conspicuous."

About fifteen minutes passed as we talked over the loud music and tried to ignore the dancers. And then, from behind the bar, another man in white slacks and blue blazer came down some stairs and out onto the floor of the club.

"We've got a positive ID on the second bouncer," I said. David turned momentarily to look.

"Yeah. He just came from the office. That's where *we* need to be."

"Two lonely men," came a female voice from behind my shoulder. "Mind if I join you?"

I turned to look at a short brunette, wearing a tight tank top and shorts that looked too short to be comfortable.

If we didn't play along, we'd be exposed, I thought. And if we did play the role, this girl might be exposed in another manner of speaking, and that was certainly not on the agenda. I looked at David, who looked as confused as I was.

"What was that plan you were working on?" I asked him.

"I forgot."

"Mind if I sub in one of my own?"

"Be my guest."

I turned to the girl, who was looking a little impatient. "We're not good company right now, what with these stinky old cigars," I said. "But do me a favor. I'll buy you a drink if you go upstairs and tell Garrett Maxwell that two customers have a complaint and want to talk to him."

"Sure," she said. I handed her a ten dollar bill, and she marched off.

A few minutes later a blazer approached our table.

"Is there something I can do for you?"

I looked at my cigar and watched the smoke curl up from it. "No, thanks. We'd rather talk to Maxwell."

"He's tied up right now. I'm afraid if you have a complaint, you'll have to talk to me about it."

"No can do, guy. Tell Mr. Maxwell that he really ought to make some time for us. An ounce of prevention is worth a kilo of cure, you know."

The bouncer's eyes darkened. This one had a dark, well-trimmed beard that accentuated his frown. He turned on his heel and walked over to the bartender, who was watching the proceedings.

A minute later he walked back to us.

"Stand," he said.

We stood.

"Arms up."

David nodded to me. I held my arms up as the bouncer frisked me. He did the same to David. Once he was assured we weren't wired or armed, he led us behind the bar and up a steep flight of stairs. Goon #2 was close behind me, leaving a waitress to watch the door. The goon at the top of the stairs knocked. After a second he opened the door, and we followed him into the room.

It was laid out like Maggie had said: a couch to the left, a door to the girls' dressing room on the right, and a desk and filing cabinets directly in front of us.

Garrett Maxwell was nothing like I'd expected.

He was a balding man in his late fifties; he looked more like a Rotary Club member than a gang leader. He was working on a ledger sheet, a ten-key calculator rumbling away, and he barely acknowledged that we were there.

Behind me Goon #2 closed the door, then locked it. I hate that sound.

"What's the matter, gentlemen?" Without looking up, he motioned to the couch, then to the ashtray on his desk. We put our cigars in the ashtray for the time being, but we didn't sit down.

Although it was supposed to be David's show, I spoke up. "Maxwell, you look like a reasonable man."

He looked up. "I consider myself so, yes. But what is your complaint?"

"Why are you trying to kill Margaret Sullivan? Isn't that a little unreasonable?"

His expressionless face found an expression: amusement.

"I don't know what you're talking about," he said. Then to his bouncers, "Did you search these gentlemen?"

"Yes, sir," said the guy with the cold hands.

"Fine. Boys, are you accusing me of a crime?"

"We're not accusing you of anything. We simply want to know why you want to kill a girl."

"I'm sorry, I can't help you."

He waved us away and turned his attention back to his ledger. I felt arms grab me from behind.

"Let's leave quietly and not disturb the other customers," Goon #2 said in my ear.

"David, I think it's time to wing it," I said.

David, with a goon holding his arms behind him as well, grinned at me. "OK, Emerson. Oops. Was I not supposed to say your name?"

"I don't think it matters at this point."

David shrugged, but then turned the downward movement of his shoulders into a sharp jab with his elbows in his captor's gut. He turned enough to catch the guy's chin with his shoulder on the way back up, just as the goon was going down. David broke loose, considered another blow, then apparently decided against overkill. The guy went down all by himself.

Maxwell was looking on, again with amusement.

Meanwhile, my own personal goon was backing away from David, keeping me in between himself and my favorite photographer. My arms were being pulled back in a pretzel-like manner — a tactic I vaguely remembered watching David use a few months earlier to convince a skinhead that although he wasn't Catholic, it was time for confession.

Pain was starting to bother me. I've never liked pain, as a rule, and I was wondering exactly what my best friend was going to do about this situation. My vision was getting a little blurry, but I saw David grin and brush his nose with the back of his hand, kind of like John Wayne did just before he called you "Pilgrim."

I remembered how much David liked John Wayne movies. It's strange what goes through your mind at moments like those.

"Emerson, a little to the right."

"Sure," I said.

"No, Emerson, the other right. My right."

"What — did you drive your tank like this? No wonder you kept driving through buildings."

"Now to the left a little. My left. OK, Emerson, now."

I threw my head back with all the strength I could gather. I felt the cartilage in Goon #2's nose crunch as his grip on my arms loosened, and I was able to break free. I turned, but he was already on his knees, holding his face.

I turned back to Maxwell, who was still smiling but was now holding a revolver.

"Very nice," he said. "My boys are Israeli-trained, but you brought a real, live Israeli. Now, what is this all about? Talk fast."

"First of all, Mr. Maxwell, David here really hates guns. I mean really."

David nodded, then reached for his cigar.

"Second, I already asked you the only question I'm interested in knowing the answer to. Tell us that, and we'll leave."

"I'm not out to kill anyone. That's the simple truth. Now you will leave."

David nodded and started to turn around to go. In mid-turn, however, he spun back around and flicked his cigar at Maxwell's face. Maxwell almost dropped the gun trying to fend off the cigar. That moment was long enough for David to roll across the desk, take Maxwell's gun hand, and gently relieve it of its burden (and most of its feeling, I was sure, after seeing the way David slammed the poor guy's elbow onto the desk — you gotta hate that).

"Reflex action," David said. "People don't like fire coming at their faces."

"I can see why," I said. "Bad for the elbows."

David took the gun and backed off, using it merely to make sure the recovering goons didn't try anything.

"Where's he staying?" I asked Maxwell, who was starting to look a little scared. His arm hung limp at his side, and he was rubbing it with his left one.

"Who?"

"The Israeli soldier who trained these goons," I said. "Come on, it's too late to play dumb. I have to hand it to you — it's a great idea. You start losing your drug war, so you bring in an expert in urban warfare. Then someone takes off with your cash and some coke, and you send him to find it and even the score."

"I sent Moshe to find it, yes, but I'm not interested in 'scores.' He's not under orders to kill anyone."

"Then he's developing an independent streak," I said. "We've been shot at twice, and an innocent girl's car was blown up. Good thing she wasn't in it or we wouldn't be here just talking."

Maxwell considered this information.

"Has she fooled you like she fooled me?"

"What do you mean?" I asked.

"She convinced me she was sincere," he said. "If she had stayed, I would have trained her to be a manager."

"What proof do you have that she took the money and the drugs?"

"Circumstantial evidence, I admit," he said. "But a lot of it. I first sent my nephew, who worked for me, to find her. I haven't heard from him for several days now, so I sent Moshe to find Brian, and if he could, to find the money and the merchandise."

"How much money are we really talking about here?" I asked. "Is that much money worth a young woman's life? He wants to kill her. We can stop him, but you've got to tell us where he is."

Maxwell sighed, took a pen and a scrap of paper, reached for a card in his Rolodex and wrote out a phone number.

"This is all I know," he said. "Moshe doesn't call me from there because I don't want the call traced back to here. He calls me from pay phones. But if I needed him back here, this is where I would reach him."

David was motioning the goons over to the couch. They were complying — slowly. I walked over and took the scrap of paper; after a second thought I took the Rolodex card as well. I grabbed Maxwell's phone and dialed the number to Sarah's cellular phone. It took a few seconds for the various uplinks and downlinks and satellites to patch me through, but eventually her phone rang. It must have gone off in her purse. She answered almost immediately; it sounded like she was in a car.

"It's Emerson," I said. "Find a pay phone and call me back at this number." I read the number off Maxwell's telephone.

"Will do."

She hung up, and we waited for about two minutes before his phone rang. Maxwell answered it calmly, then handed it to me.

"Is everything OK, sweetie?" Sarah inquired ever so politely.

"It's fine here," I said. "Your pigeon is at this telephone number."

I gave her the number off the Rolodex card.

"Thanks, sweetheart. I'll take it from here. Cover your exit, boys."

"You bet we will. See you in about four hours."

I hung up, then looked at the phone. "By the way, Maxwell, did Trish get Maggie's message?"

"Maggie?"

"Margaret, or Meagan as she was known here. I know it gets confusing."

"I haven't seen Trish for a few days, but I'm sure she'll get it. So Margaret hasn't broken all her ties? She didn't seem to mind dropping Brian."

"I'm sure he'll recover."

"Probably," Maxwell said. "He always had a few others on deck and ready to step up to the plate, as it were."

"A baseball metaphor," I said. "I think I could begin to like you, Maxwell."

"I'm deeply touched."

"We're going to leave now, Mr. Maxwell," I said patiently. "Keep your boys calm and quiet and no police ever have to know we were here."

David looked almost compassionate. "You'd better see someone about your nose," he said to the goon holding a bloodied handkerchief to his face. "That looks like a bad break. Want me to set it for you until you can see a doctor?"

The goon just glared.

"I was only trying to help," David said. He handed me the gun and motioned for me to go down first.

We backed out of the room, and David lingered by the door until I got down the stairs, past the bar, and over to the entrance. I had a pretty good bead on the office doorway, so I covered it until David caught up with me. We left the building quickly, got into the Jeep with David driving, and sped off down the highway.

"What do you think he'll do?" I asked.

"Wonder where we came from," he said. "He knows we're not police, but this might make him nervous enough to shut down for a little while — his drugs, not his bar."

"Sarah told us not to jeopardize the narcotics investigation," I said. "I guess we blew that."

"Maybe," he said. "Maybe not."

15

We drove for the next hour or so in silence. I knew that Sarah had the resources to find an address that went along with the phone number we'd obtained for her. If Maxwell didn't contact this Moshe guy first, Sarah and whatever backup she had would have a good shot at picking him up.

I hoped they'd wait for us, though. I wanted to actually see them — whoever "they" turned out to be — bust the guy who was trying to kill Maggie.

It was almost midnight when we drove back into town and went straight to Remington's apartment, the newest command bunker in a war I was just beginning to understand. Sarah, Remington, and Maggie were all awake and waiting for us.

Sarah had her purse slung over her shoulder as she let us in. At first I wondered where she was going. Then I saw a silver glint from what I knew was a large-caliber Israeli pistol, and I knew she'd just been playing it safe.

"Hello, girls," I said. "Did you miss us?"

"Most dreadfully," Sarah said. "So much so that we had to go clean out the malls. Emerson, we found some new curtains for your little house; the last set was a little damaged by the incident last night. A. C. picked the new ones out, but I'm afraid you'll have to get rid of that couch now. It simply won't work with the curtains."

"Fine," I said. "That's the landlord's couch anyway. He'd just left it there for lack of anywhere to store it. He didn't want to leave it in the barn."

"The barn is exactly where it belongs," she said. "Now, I have some ideas about what we can do with the kitchen. I've talked them over with A. C. and Maggie, and they agree."

"Hold it," I said. "You're switching too fast for me, lady. You've got to let me know when you're being a commando and when you're being a frustrated interior decorator. Don't you want to tell us about our friend Moshe?"

"You know his name?"

"Only his first name. Why?"

"Just curious. It's never good to know too much."

"You're talking to a reporter, Sarah. I *always* want to know too much. I think it stems from some kind of brain damage in my youth."

"Indubitably," Remington said.

"No comments from the audience, please," I responded. "Now, Sarah, where did that number trace back to?"

"A hotel room here in town," she said.

"Which hotel?"

"The Holiday Inn."

I was given no opportunity to ask further questions and barely got to say hello to Maggie and Remington before my photographer friend and I were kicked out of the slumber party and sent on our separate ways. David drove off toward his house, where Mordechai would be waiting up to hear the details. I went home to my apartment.

Climbing up the stairs I realized how tired I was. Fooling around with guns and goons and long drives all weekend takes a lot out of a guy. I unlocked my door and went into my apartment — all the more lonely because Airborne, though at least in town, was not here to greet me. What did greet me was the flashing light on my answering machine. I hesitated fearfully, then hit the Play button as I reached over and opened my cupboard and found a bagel in the bread box.

"Dunn, this is Singer," the machine informed me. "It's Sunday afternoon, about 4 P.M. I just saw the report on the drive-by at your new place."

"It wasn't a drive-by," I told the machine. "He had to get out of his car to do it."

"Call the station when you get in if you want some police protection. Or call me at home. I'll come baby-sit you and your new girlfriend."

"She ain't my new girlfriend, you flatfoot," I replied with a mouthful of bagel and bad grammar.

"Dunn, I don't know what you've gotten us into, but it seems to be getting out of hand. Call me when you get in."

I dialed Singer's home number. He answered almost immediately.

"Yeah," he said, obviously awake.

"This is Emerson. You rang?"

"You've lived through another day, I see. I'm glad to hear that. What's going on, Dunn?"

I sat down at the kitchen table and sighed. "We're out of our league, Bill," I said. "Here's the deal. The fat old man and the nice old lady at the jewelry store — you remember them, right?"

"Yeah."

"They're not a fat old man and a nice old lady."

"Then what are they?"

"I don't know for sure, but I have some suspicions. What has Sally told you about the sting operation in Nueces County?"

"Most of the major points."

"Did she mention a drug-related gang war?"

"Yeah, but those go on all the time."

"Did she mention that one side was winning?"

Singer paused. "I think she did. Yes . . . She mentioned an incident three weeks ago; one faction hit a house used as a distribution point by the other faction."

"Then let me guess. The first faction, the aggressors, were Maxwell's bunch, right?"

"Right."

"And the second was a group of wanna-be Crips. Maxwell's guys hit the house with military precision, didn't they? Took out the principals and left a few alive to warn the rest of the gang."

"Have you been reading the police reports?"

"No, I'm just guessing. Maxwell realized a few months ago that he was losing ground to this other gang. So like any other good businessman, he hired a consultant to come in and help him make his operation more efficient. Specifically, he hired an Israeli soldier to come in and train his 'lieutenants' to fight and win."

"I don't know how deep into the operation Sally and the task force was able to get," Singer said after a moment. "From what she told me, this might be news to them. They've got foreigners going in and out of there all the time — mostly Colombian and Ecuadorian tourists, if you know what I mean. But this Israeli aspect would explain a lot."

"The problem is, he's not down there training the lieutenants right now. He's up here trying to kill Maggie and get Maxwell's merchandise back."

Singer was silent for a moment. "There were Feds in the office tonight; they'd come in from Houston. They took over the chief's office and his secure phone line. So this is what it's all about."

"I guess so. But it's about the Israeli, not Maggie."

"Dunn, does she have the drugs? Or the cash?"

"Not that I know of, unless they were stashed in her car — her late car. What about her hotel room? She never went back to it after her car was bombed. Did you guys find anything there?"

"Nothing. A suitcase with a few clothes; it's still sitting in my office, waiting for her to pick it up. We found nothing else. She didn't even have a hotel towel stashed in her suitcase."

"I told you she was honest."

"Honest? Then why is some Israeli in my city trying to kill her and anyone else within range?"

"Well, Bill, I haven't figured that part out yet. But as soon as I do, I'll let you know. I promise."

"Look, Dunn. I'm getting more information from you than I am from my own brass. And the Feds certainly weren't talking tonight. With them involved, I can't act without orders. But I want you to call me if you learn anything more, or if anything like last night's shotgun attack happens again."

"Like I said, buddy, we're out of our league. But I'll call you."

He hung up, and I leaned back to ponder it all. The Feds' involvement explained why Sarah was so disinterested in a report from us — or to us — when we got back earlier. My guess was that the Feds already had Moshe's hotel room — if not Moshe himself — under surveillance.

Half an hour later I was in bed, quickly drifting off, glad of the fact that Monday would be a light day at work.

The next thing I knew the phone was ringing.

"Hello?" I answered groggily. I squinted at the clock; it was almost midnight.

"Is this Emerson Dunn?" It was a female's voice. After a moment I recognized it as Trish's voice. She was probably returning Maggie's call.

"Yeah, this is Emerson," I said. "Trish?"

"Yes. Can I see you? For just a few minutes? I know you can't tell me where Meagan is, but I need to talk to you about her."

"Here? You're not in Corpus?"

"No, I'm in town. Nearby, as a matter of fact. I'm at a gas station near your office."

"Sure, come on by. I'll be ready."

She hung up, and I wondered how she got my address. She must have found it in the telephone book; simple enough after I'd given her my name, I guess. I got up and dressed. I was buttoning my shirt when a knock came at the door. I battened down all remaining hatches and answered the door.

A slender woman with dark eyes and jet-black hair stood under the awning.

"Trish?"

She nodded and came in. She looked around the room for a moment while I closed the door and turned toward her.

"What is it you need to talk about?"

"Meagan. I'm worried. Some bad people are after her. Do you know where she is now? I need to know. I need to warn her." She sounded desperate.

"Don't get so worked up," I said. "It's under control. We know all about the bad folks, and we're taking appropriate measures." I was starting to sound like a city official discussing a drainage problem.

Trish's dark eyes were still darting around the room, as if she were looking for a way out. "I need to know," she repeated. "I need to warn her."

"Can I get you anything?"

"Coffee."

I nodded and went to the kitchen. I found a jar of instant coffee and put a mug of water into the microwave. After a minute the water was boiling, so I took it out and spooned some granules of instant into it. It looked about the right color, so I called out to Trish, "Cream or sugar?"

Her voice came from my living room. "Nothing. I've changed my mind."

I stared at the coffee for a moment, then left it. I went back into the living room and found Trish heading for the door.

"I've got to go," she said. "Tell Meagan I'll be in touch. And tell her to get out of here. She's not safe here. I care about what happens to her, no matter what you think."

"What do I think?" I asked.

"You don't trust me. That's OK. That's probably best for her. I just came to warn her. Do it for me."

She said nothing else as she left. I went back to bed, wondering what that was all about. I drifted off to sleep again, only to once again be awakened by the phone.

"Emerson, my good friend," came Mordechai's big voice. "It's the middle of the morning. What are you still doing in bed? If I try this, my sister — she will bang the pots and the pans. She never, ever will let me sleep late. And look where it's gotten me."

I grunted.

"Come to the jewelry store. We will have some fun today, yes?"

"I have to work today," I said.

"Yes, yes, work. Another thing my sister talks much about. She says I never do it. But that is only because I am smart."

"Well, I've got to do it. For a few hours at least."

I looked at the clock; it said 10:14 A.M. I knew there was no rush to get in to the office, but I figured the sooner I did, the sooner I could get out.

"If I go to work now, Mordechai, I can come to your shop after about 6 P.M."

"That will do."

I almost expected the old colonel to say, "Carry on, son." But he didn't. Lurking behind that disarming friendliness and those dumb jokes was a very shrewd mind. Maybe he just liked my company, but I figured a more plausible explanation was that he was up to something. Hopefully they'd picked up Moshe, or at least had a bead on him.

Realizing the utter futility of trying to figure Mordechai out, I showered and found some amazingly clean clothes to wear to the office. That's always a good thing — wearing clean clothes to the office.

The day went slowly. The office was crowded but not with reporters. Sherri and Robert were out gathering news or cruising the garage sales, whichever seemed most entertaining. Since it was summer we didn't have a sports staff (these days we usually used a new intern from the University of Houston each semester — they work cheap). Even Louise was gone, off at a meeting at the corporate office. Everyone from advertising, classifieds, and circulation was there, but they weren't interested in spending quality time with me, so I got away with not actually having to interact with anyone except Sharon, our receptionist.

"Any more gossip on this mysterious blonde?" she asked. "I'm getting more and more reports on my own. You'd better come clean before I start believing some of them."

"I deny everything," I said.

"I knew you would. Just checking."

"On behalf of Remington, whom you people almost have me married off to, I thank you from the bottom of my heart."

I wrote a quick editorial or two for the Thursday paper we'd be putting together on Tuesday night and opened mail for a couple of hours — I'd gotten a little behind. A little? Have you ever seen Mount Everest? At lunchtime I ran across the street to the drugstore and had a BLT at the lunch counter with a bunch of men at least twice my age (a couple of them were more than three times my age, well into their nineties). They were grousing about The State of Things, from the President to the mayor to crime. I listened politely and ate.

I went back to the office and found Robert and Sherri there, working hard and looking as if they needed very little guidance. I was getting discouraged and depressed about my lessening importance in the grand scheme of things. I even found a complete story budget from each of them on my desk. I was just slipping into a pit of temporary depression when the phone rang. I was really beginning to hate Bell's marvelous invention.

"Newsroom."

"Dunn, the Feds are backing off. But they're waiting in reserve, with a lot of firepower. And a group of us locals are on stand-by. Whatever your friends are going to do, they're going to do it soon."

"What do you mean, the Feds are backing off?"

"That's just what we were told. Dunn, this is something international. Are you still involved?"

"Yeah. Tonight."

"Come by my office beforehand."

"Sure. See you at about 5 P.M. then."

"I'll be here."

I tried for a while to distract Robert and Sherri from their work. We talked about The State of Things for a while, just like the old men at the drugstore. For the most part, we all seemed to agree. Politicians and crime — we were against them.

And then the door opened, and Brian walked in with the photo of Maggie.

He didn't seem to notice me at first. He was halted in his tracks by Sharon, the world's best and most dangerous receptionist. He'd have to explain his business before he was allowed to proceed into the newsroom. Brian looked a little tired, as if he really had been working during the days and searching the bars at night.

"I'm looking for an old girlfriend," he said to Sharon, holding out Maggie's photo. "I don't want to go into my life story, but she might need me. I figured you guys at a newspaper would know who comes and goes."

"Brian . . ." I said.

He looked over at me with sluggish recognition.

"Is this the newspaper you work at?"

"Yeah," I said. "No luck yet?"

"No. I figured you worked for the Galveston paper."

"No."

"Well, how about you? Any sign of her? I'm pretty sure she's around here someplace. My old boss said he got a tip. I talked to him this morning."

That meant Maxwell might have said something about David and me.

"Sorry," I said.

Brian walked over to my desk, looking at the brass name plate Remington had given me when I was promoted.

"Emerson Dunn . . ." Brian said. "Never heard of you. I must not be reading the right newspapers."

He smiled; it wasn't unfriendly.

"I thought you'd have given up by now," I said.

"The more I think about it, the more I think I miss her," he said. "Maybe she's worth another shot."

I didn't mention to Brian that people had been taking shots at his girlfriend all week. "Maybe. If you find her, then what?"

"I think I can square things with my old boss," he said. "He seemed to have backed off a little already. He didn't seem so interested in getting even. With him off our backs, we might just sail away. I'm thinking about Jamaica now. The dollar is doing pretty good over there."

"Sounds like a nice plan," I said. "But how can you square things with your boss? You said before that she's stolen something."

"Yeah, well, I didn't tell you one thing about my old boss. He's my uncle. I'll tell him to take it out of my inheritance or something. If I ask him, he won't hurt her. He might want her to work part of it off, but we could do that for a few months and then sail south. Doesn't matter to me."

I studied him. I could tell from his eyes he really did care about finding Maggie. I still didn't know if Maggie cared to be found.

"Like I said, I'll tell her where you are if I see her," I said.

"Thanks. And look, here's a phone number. I got a phone hooked up to my boat at the slip now."

Brian walked out, smiling at Sharon as he left. Robert and Sherri just looked at me.

"Was he looking for your blonde?" Sharon asked.

"She's not my blonde," I said.

"He seems OK," Sherri piped up. "I like the idea of sailing away. He was cute too."

"Yeah, well, you're almost engaged, so you just watch out," I said.

"I'm no closer to it than you, and you've been running around with a blonde all week."

"I soundly deny any and all accusations."

At about 3:30 P.M. David walked in. I hadn't seen him or a photo budget all day, so I asked what he had in mind for front-page art.

"I got some good shots of football practice at the high school this morning," he said.

I nodded; it would make a good end-of-summer type of shot — football teams already practicing for the coming season. Not that ours would win any games, but this town was far too loyal to let a few on-field embarrassments diminish its support for its high-school heroes.

For another hour I presided over my dominion without much effort or usefulness. David finished running his film and emerged from the darkroom, still wearing his apron. As he was taking it off (and replacing it with his beloved photographer's vest), he asked in a roundabout way if I'd made any plans for the evening.

"Your uncle seems to have made them for me," I said. "I'm supposed to meet him at his jewelry store after a while."

David just nodded, then gathered his gear and left.

"Well, since no one seems to care whether I exist or not, I'm leaving," I said to my staff and to Sharon.

"Fine," Robert said. "Can I have your chair?"

"I don't mean leaving for good," I replied. "Just for the night."

Sherri voiced a cheery good-bye (that cheeriness could really get on your nerves; at least Robert was as cynical as me). I left the building and got into my Ford. I was almost to my apartment before I remembered I'd promised to meet Singer. I turned down a side street and made my way back to the police station.

The dispatcher buzzed me in, and I found Singer sitting behind his desk, looking over some daily shift reports.

"You wanted to see me, Principal Bill?"

"I just want to give you a word of warning."

"And what might that word be?"

"It's written down."

He pushed a large, bumpy manila envelope toward me.

"In here," he said.

I picked up the envelope, and as soon as I felt its heaviness I realized it didn't hold paperwork.

"What's this?" I asked innocently.

"Against department procedures, I'm sure," he said. "But take it. You borrowed it for target practice, remember that. There's also a box of ammo — jacketed hollowpoints. Should do the job."

I opened the envelope and looked down at Singer's old .38 special police revolver. He had an automatic now, and I hadn't seen this one in months. I also saw the box of ammo. I put the envelope down.

"Thanks, but no thanks," I said. "I can't do it."

"Do you know what you're getting into?"

"I have no idea."

"Neither do I," he said. "But I'd sure hate for the county medical examiner to be picking shotgun pellets out of your vital organs tonight."

"What a touching thing to say, Bill. I didn't know you cared."

"Take it."

"I can't."

"Fine. I tried," he said. He looked a little resigned to it; he probably hadn't expected me to take his gun anyway.

"But, Dunn, call me if you get into any trouble. I know David's a good man to have at your side, but this is serious."

"I'll call."

I left his office with him still staring at me. Once again I had that terrible feeling that he knew something I didn't.

I looked at my watch once I got out to my car. It was almost 6 P.M. I didn't really need to run by my apartment, so I drove up Commerce Street to Mordechai's shop. It was after-hours, so he was alone; I went in through an unlocked door and discovered he was on the telephone. He muttered something in Hebrew and hung up.

"Emerson, it is good to see you. The glass in your new house was fixed today; I saw to it myself. And you, my friend, you look well."

"Yeah, but will I be well after tonight? What's the plan, Mordechai? You move on Moshe tonight, don't you?"

His face got serious again.

"Yes. But everything is taken care of. Sarah and I worked it out; you may think of it as a free dinner."

It didn't sound like an ordinary invitation.

16

An hour and a half later I was in Remington's apartment as Mordechai and Sarah laid out the plan for Remington, Maggie, and me. I had driven Mordechai to my girlfriend's apartment; we found Remington on the couch with Maggie, and Sarah in the kitchen — making cookies or something. She was checking the oven as we entered. Amazing! The woman was Mata Hari and Julia Child all in one.

It was to be a simple dinner. All we had to do was be sitting ducks for a man with a shotgun. But at least we were getting free schnitzel out of it.

"Maggie and Emerson will drive to the restaurant," Mordechai said, "driving Emerson's very unique car slowly past the Holiday Inn. He is there now. When your car — which is in need of a new muffler, I think you should know — goes by his window, he will come out. And as he follows you to the restaurant, we will take care of him."

"Why not just bust him now? You know where he is," Remington asked.

"No way," I said. "The whole point of this exercise is to avoid an international incident. No publicity, no police, and no loud breaking-and-enterings. No kicked-in doors, no disturbed guests in nearby rooms. Am I right?"

Mordechai grunted. "We must also get him out of his hotel

room — we don't know what weapons he has in there. We suspect explosives, of course. So we bring him out, onto our ground, and take care of him then."

"What do you mean, 'take care of him'?" Remington asked.

"Not to worry — we will reason with him," Sarah said.

"Sure you will," I said. "So when do we go?"

"Hold it," Remington said. "Let's get the 'we' part straightened out. Maggie's not going."

Mordechai looked serious again. He didn't like to be questioned.

"I did some shopping today," Remington said. "Take a look at this."

Remington pulled a Marilyn Monroe-style wig from her purse. Mordechai frowned. So did I.

"Forget it, boys," Remington said. "Maggie and I are the same size — those are my clothes she's wearing. A little makeup work, and if we keep the lights in the restaurant a little low, he'll never know. And besides, you'll probably have him as soon as he walks out the door."

"Why?" Maggie asked, speaking up for the first time since I'd entered.

"Because it's my turn now," Remington said after a pause. "My turn to take someone's place. I can do it, Sarah."

She appealed her case to the older woman with a look.

"If you want to, honey, it's fine with me," Sarah said after a pause. "But if this gets out of control, you two are to duck out the back. The Schmidt boys already have their instructions."

Half an hour later I found myself praying fervently as I drove down Commerce to the restaurant. The woman seated next to me was calm, beautiful, and most definitely Remington. I felt better. Maggie was still an unknown commodity. I knew Remington well enough to know how she'd react if "things got out of hand."

We passed the hotel. I saw a couple of rental cars and a few out-of-state plates, but no sign of Mordechai's Buick or Sarah's Jeep.

It all seemed so simple. A calm, well-planned exercise to flush out our Israeli target.

But when the local cops and the federal agents had backed off, it was ultimately up to us to do the job. That bothered me. Why weren't there federal agents on every corner and in the hotel, dressed as tree trimmers and street cleaners and bankers and waiters and desk clerks?

Because relations were currently tense, I knew. The State Department probably had given Israel a certain amount of time to take care of its own renegade soldier, to whisk him away as if he'd never been in this country.

I drove slowly past the hotel, halfway expecting our windows to be taken out by a shotgun blast on our way by. But nothing happened. There was no sign of movement. All the doors remained closed; no curtains were pushed aside, as far as I could see anyway.

Maybe it wouldn't happen tonight. Maybe our target was out of town — up in Houston or back down in Nueces County.

"Emerson, I haven't seen much of you lately," Remington said, reaching out and taking my hand. "Not really, at least."

"Yeah. That's been a problem. I've missed you."

"Me too."

"Are we back to that? I thought we'd advanced beyond the 'Me too' stage."

She laughed. I watched her face; it had too much makeup (she rarely wore much), and the wig did more than I would have expected. From any distance at all, she would be mistaken for Margaret Sullivan. Certainly through the picture-window glass of the restaurant, even as spotless as Walter and Gunther kept it, she couldn't be distinguished from Maggie. The hair color was a little off, Remington's chin was different, but the right shading here and the right color of eyeshadow did the trick.

"Remington, this is a really brave thing you're doing."

"You too. They didn't really need us, you know. Maggie could have cooperated with them and just gone to the restaurant by herself."

"Then why did they involve civilians?"

"I think Sarah is worried about Maggie. The poor girl has a lot to sort through these days; a lot is on her mind. She was willing to do it, but Sarah said she couldn't be counted on to react well, to duck in time if anything happened. To react well means you have to want to live, to really want it deep down inside, Sarah said. Any hesitation about that and you're lost."

"I guess I agree."

We found the restaurant parking lot empty — the boys had apparently cleared their customers out a little early.

We walked into the restaurant just as we had for Remington's birthday just a few nights before. So much had happened since then. Walter wordlessly led us to a booth, one against the picture window facing the street. Anyone looking for a reporter and his blonde bombshell buddy would have no trouble spotting us. A couple of shotgun blasts through that window and we'd be a problem no longer.

But that fact kept bothering me; what were Mordechai and Sarah doing putting us in this position? I just couldn't believe they thought of us as expendable participants in some game of international intrigue. I actually think the old Jewish soldier and his Mad Realtor sidekick liked us. Hopefully that meant the mysterious Moshe would be intercepted long before he got within shotgun range. Instead of listening for squealing car tires or an approaching auto, I realized it might be wiser to listen for a few gunshots up the road a ways, closer to the Holiday Inn than to us.

"Please have a seat. I am sorry there is no silverware to greet you, but we are having problems with our new dishwasher," Walter said stiffly. Then he leaned over a little.

"It's an Israeli-made model, a very temperamental machine,"

he added with a grin. "But don't worry, I will make it work. I have promised schnitzel."

Remington looked a little confused.

"Don't worry about it too much," I told her as Walter turned on a heel and marched off. "That means David's in the kitchen, and Walter's making him wash dishes. As well he should."

David was as regular here as I was, and he and Walter would sit up at night arguing world politics until David was laughing hysterically and Walter was red in the face. They both thought the world of each other, but I'm sure Walter couldn't pass up this chance at less-than-divine retribution.

That also confirmed my theory that if Moshe was going to be taken out, it was planned to happen up the block from us. Leaving David Ben Zadok in the kitchen — probably unarmed, knowing David — was likely Mordechai's way of making us feel safe. But he had no intention of letting Moshe get too close.

A few moments later the lights were lowered, just as they had been for Remington's birthday dinner. Walter came back out, followed closely by Gunther (who was not wearing an apron, obviously delighted to give his duties to someone else for a change).

"The usual, I presume?" Walter said.

"Sure," Remington said. "But no coffee for me. I'm already a little jumpy."

Gunther looked sympathetic. I was sure both of these guys complied willingly with any requests Mordechai — or more probably Sarah Tate — made of them, even if it meant their restaurant might become a shooting gallery.

Gunther had brought out glasses of water, along with spotless silverware. He laid them out in front of us.

"We will be in the back if you need anything," he said regretfully. "That is not our choice."

The brothers walked slowly to the kitchen.

"What next?" Remington asked.

I looked into her eyes; she was worried.

"Lighten up, Aggie," I said, hoping the strain in my own voice didn't show. "You know, if I were ever to stop calling you by your last name, I'm afraid I'd have to call you Aggie."

"I think not," she smiled sweetly. "Your mother told me what you were called for the first few years of your life, remember? I believe you were called 'Sonny.' Isn't that correct? You wouldn't want that generally made known, would you?"

"You don't fight fair."

"I've been thinking, though, that 'A. C.' is a little too formal, a little too distant. I used to like that, but now . . . Maybe I'll go by Cathy, since my middle name is Catherine."

"Isn't Catherine your mother's name also?"

"Yes, but she's much too proper to go by Cathy. I might do that. Could you adjust?"

"Sure, but I might slip now and then."

A few moments later our dinners arrived. Still no gunshots.

We talked about Airborne. Still no gunshots.

We finished up with some strudel that Gunther brought us — with the demand that we tell him, after we partook of it, who made it — him or Walter.

"Definitely David," I said, chewing a mouthful of it. "It's stringy, tastes a little like a throw rug, and reeks of stale dark-room chemicals. All in all, one of the best dishes you boys have forced upon us in months."

Gunther laughed. "You are right — it isn't mine. It is Walter's. I will relay to him your compliments."

"Don't do that," Remington pleaded. "Don't set him off. You know how he gets."

Still no gunshots, not even from the kitchen.

That thought was at the forefront of my mind even as we sipped our after-dinner coffee, waiting for a crescendo we couldn't prepare for. What would happen? Would Moshe slip through and get a clear shot at us? Or would he be dragged into the restaurant by Feds and Mossad agents and a lady with big hair? Would Bill Singer be investigating any extra deaths in the morning? If so, whose?

No answers came. Time passed. I looked at my watch; it was after 10 P.M.

"The fish aren't biting," I said. "I say we pack it up. If we don't get out of here soon, I'm going to start liking that blonde look on you."

"Then let's go." Remington's voice sounded almost relieved. "I'm a brunette for life."

"I'll take you home," I said.

I announced out loud to the kitchen that we were going. I saw David pop his head out to grin at us. He apparently didn't spend the evening trying to cultivate his own set of world-class ulcers, as we did. He waved but said nothing.

I left some money on the table and led Remington to the door. As I opened it I looked both ways. They teach you that in school. Nothing. The street was quiet, as it should be on a Monday night. A patrol car passed at a usual rate of speed; the officer in it seemed completely uninterested in us.

I walked Remington to my car and subtly checked the back-seat as I unlocked her door. Nothing. I got in on my side. Nothing. A terrible thought occurred to me as I started the car, but when nothing blew up I felt a little better. No, I felt a lot better. I pulled out onto the street, looking in my mirrors, watching parking lots and oncoming traffic.

Nothing.

As we neared Remington's apartment I started to breathe normally.

"I sure hope we don't have to do this again," I said. "The food was good, but the ambiance left a little to be desired tonight."

"Yeah." Remington scooted over in the seat toward me. "What did you mean when you said you might have to stop calling me by my last name?"

She grinned a little, adding emphasis to her evil motives. I thought once more of that jet bound for anywhere, any country that doesn't have a good extradition treaty with the U.S. or reliable phone lines.

"I said *might*," I replied.

"You say a lot of things over romantic dinners," she said. "Remember?"

"Yup. But I wouldn't call tonight romantic. It was a little stressful. But yeah, I remember what all I get myself into during these things."

"Any regrets?"

"Naw," I said.

"Such a way with words."

We pulled into her apartment complex. There was no sign of any familiar cars, except Remington's. Sarah Tate's Jeep was gone, as was Mordechai's Buick.

"I guess they whisked Maggie off to another safe house," I said. "Maybe they left a note."

I walked Remington up the stairs and used her key to unlock the door.

As she started to walk in, I noticed that the apartment wasn't empty. My night was taking a turn for the worse.

Margaret Sullivan, a.k.a. Maggie, a.k.a. Meagan, was sitting very upright in a chair. Beside her, standing with pistol in hand, was a dark Middle Easterner with casual American clothes and a dangerous calmness in his manner. He was smaller than David but had a look of intensity about him.

"Come in," he said, waving the pistol at me. "Bring in your girlfriend as well."

I hesitated and thought of stiff-arming Remington back out of the way and simply shutting the door. The thought didn't last long; I realized Maggie would still be on the other side of the door.

Moshe seemed a teeny bit impatient as he waved the gun at Maggie.

"Come in now," he said. "You're wasting my time."

The implied threat was there. Remington had seen it and pushed her way through. I followed grudgingly.

"Hello, Moshe," I said. I could see that Maggie wasn't bound or bleeding. She looked a little frightened, but she didn't appear hurt.

"Hello, Mr. Dunn. Forgive the intrusion."

"Oh, it's not my apartment. I think you should apologize to the lady here."

He bowed slightly at Remington. "Please forgive me. I do not enjoy doing business this way."

He leaned against the couch that sat off to the side of the apartment's small living room. He was facing the door and the chair where Maggie sat.

Remington had a strange expression; she took off the wig and freed her long brown hair.

"I guess I don't need this anymore," she said.

She ran her fingers through her hair, straightening it and pulling it back some. With a little more confidence she added, "Now get out of my apartment."

"I am very sorry," Moshe said. "I know this is an inconvenience to you. I know you must be frightened. But I must get some information."

"For a jerk waving a gun around, you sure are polite," I said.

"I said I do not like doing business this way. But I have orders."

"From Maxwell? He's not backing you any longer," I said. "He ratted on you. We know your name, your Holiday Inn room number, everything. But I guess you spies and terrorists must be used to that sort of thing."

I was deliberately baiting him; he was much too calm and collected for my tastes. I at least wanted to rattle him a little.

"I am neither a terrorist nor a spy," he said, looking me straight in the eyes. "I am a soldier."

"And what information do you want?" Remington asked, approaching Maggie. Moshe didn't seem to mind. Remington knelt down and took Maggie's hand.

"I want to know where Mr. Maxwell's money is . . . And his product. Then I will go. No one will be hurt."

"That's what they all say," I replied. "Why didn't you follow us to the restaurant?"

"I almost did. But the disguise was sloppy. Meagan danced in high heels for years, but Ms. Remington had trouble coming down the stairs in them."

"I always wear flats," Remington said apologetically. "I'm not used to high heels."

"Very observant," I said. "So has Meagan — or Maggie, which is her real name — given you the information you've requested?"

"I'm afraid not."

"Hmmm. What's next?" I asked.

"Maybe you will help her remember?"

"Don't count on it," I said. "My suggestion is that you take Remington's suggestion and leave."

He turned to me and smiled. "I'm sorry, but that isn't possible."

He turned his attention back to the two women. "Please, Meagan, tell me where these things are. You say you don't know, and maybe you are telling the truth. Maybe it was an accounting error. But I find that hard to believe. What am I to do? Where is it? If I can't take it back, I must take you back."

"I don't know where it is," she said, dropping her eyes. "I told you that."

"Maggie, don't bother to talk to this guy," I said. I was still standing near the door. I took a step in his direction. His gun hand immediately aimed at my chest without moving his eyes from Maggie.

"Mr. Dunn, please stay there. I will leave soon." I heard the click of a gun's safety being switched off.

But the sound came from behind me.

"Drop the gun, Captain."

Mordechai's firm voice came from the doorway, which I'd left open. If a gun battle was about to begin, I was smack-dab in the middle of it. How do I do it? I thought about how nice it would have been to be sitting down, preferably on that jet plane bound for some other country.

Moshe's eyes got a little bigger; his composure was starting to show signs of weakening.

Another order came from Mordechai, this one in Hebrew.

Moshe slowly lowered the weapon. My heart started beating again.

"What charges, Colonel?" Moshe said in English, apparently in answer to Mordechai.

"Not here," Mordechai said.

I could figure it out though.

It all fit. A relatively small drug operation in Nueces County, Texas, finds itself an Israeli soldier to train its dealers, who were losing ground to a self-styled gang with more guns and more guts. But having an Israeli turn a bunch of dealers into deadly soldiers on the wrong side of the battle is bad public relations for Israel. Naturally they're going to send someone in to extricate him.

Mordechai entered the apartment, still holding a small pistol. Sarah Tate followed closely behind him, carrying a small bag. While Mordechai held his gun on Moshe, Sarah took a small vial and a syringe from the bag. She loaded up a few cc's of something and approached Moshe.

"We're taking you home, Moshe," she said.

He nodded and looked at the needle.

"Must you use that?" the apprehended loose cannon asked.

"No," came Mordechai's voice. "Not now. I think I trust you. Give Emerson your gun."

I accepted the black automatic from the Israeli, who was suddenly looking humble. Tears were welling up in his eyes. I'd forgotten that their culture finds it more acceptable to cry than ours does. I almost wanted to hug the guy. He wasn't even as old as me and was apparently already in a whole lot of trouble. Mordechai looked solemn, as if what faced Moshe back in Israel wasn't going to be pleasant. Probably a military court martial, with little press and little hope of probation.

David walked in a second later. He took in the situation immediately and went over to Moshe.

"Come with me," David said. "We will take you to an airplane on a private airfield. It isn't far."

Moshe nodded. He started following David out the door, then looked apologetically at Maggie.

"Please forgive me," he said. "I was following orders. I would not have hurt you. You were one of the few here I liked. You remember what I gave you? When you said you were afraid going home at night? I did not like Maxwell, but he was my boss."

Maggie didn't respond. I paused for a second as well. I'd never thought of Moshe as anything but a cold-blooded killer attempting to blow away my friends and my house. Now he seemed like a lost young man — a smart young man maybe, but one who didn't have much education or even much of a future outside the military in Israel's depressed economy. He was a good soldier though. He took orders well and respected authority, and it was probably his recognition that Mordechai outranked him that prevented a gun battle.

David led Moshe out the door and down the stairs.

"Emerson, I will be back in a few hours," Mordechai said. "Sarah will not. She will return to Israel with Moshe."

"Are you going to be staying here for long?" I asked him.

"For good. That was my price. I am retired, so I did not come cheaply. Now I will live the good life with my family in America."

I smiled. So did Remington, who was still beside Maggie, holding the girl's hand.

"We will go now," Mordechai said. Sarah smiled at Maggie and Remington but said nothing. She left the apartment first.

Mordechai was almost out the door when he stopped.

"Please . . . the weapon," he said to me.

I handed him the gun with a grin. "I don't want it," I said. "These things are too loud for me."

Mordechai smiled and this time left successfully.

When the door was closed, I turned to look at Remington, who was helping Maggie up.

"So that's it? That's all there is to it? I didn't even break a sweat," I said. "One international crisis averted, painlessly and professionally."

"Right," Remington said. "At least it's over."

"Yeah," I said. But I had the feeling it wasn't. Something still wasn't right.

18

The proverbial fly in the ointment continued buzzing throughout that night. I went home — to the new house, to be with Airborne. I had to stop by my old apartment first, to gather a few things, and to Martin's to retrieve said dog, so it took about an hour to arrive. I went to sleep, knowing that I didn't know everything. The next morning I went into the office and wandered into the darkroom, looking for photos so I could decide what my front page would look like.

The darkroom said it all. A photographer's haven, a darkroom is usually best viewed in just that, the dark. They're almost always as unkempt as a reporter's desk. But not David's darkroom. It was a wreck when we hired him, and he spent an entire weekend cleaning it. Now the floors remained spotless despite the volume of liquid developing chemicals he processed every week. The shelves were kept neat; everything was always in order. I asked him about it once, and he'd shrugged. It was the army, he said. You don't do anything in a sloppy manner in the Israeli Defense Forces.

And if you were trained by the IDF, you don't make pipe bombs that don't explode at the right time, you don't shoot at windows with shotguns and simply hope someone catches a pellet, and you certainly don't conduct the sort of terror campaign waged against Maggie during the last few days.

It wasn't Moshe. Moshe had waited, had bided his time until he could get Maggie alone. He was exact, he was precise, he even surrendered in a formal, orderly manner.

I was standing in the darkroom when David entered.

"Dave, it wasn't Moshe. Would Moshe use a shotgun?"

"That's what I was thinking, Emerson. You have any assignments for me?"

"Not this morning."

"Then let's go see Brian."

19

I called Remington before we left. She had decided to take the day off from work. Maggie was still asleep on her couch. I asked Remington to keep Maggie at her apartment, behind a locked and chained door, until I called.

I also telephoned my favorite cop, Detective Sergeant Bill Singer.

"Singer," he grunted, almost cheerfully.

"Good morning," I said. "It's Dunn. Listen, I think we may still have a problem."

"The Feds said everything's taken care of."

"Everything they know about. But what if there's an extra bad actor?"

"It's possible, I suppose."

"I think I know who it is — Maggie's old boyfriend. He's on a boat in a slip in the Galveston Yacht Basin. David and I are going down there."

"You're going to see a man you two suspect of blowing holes into buildings?"

"Well, I hadn't thought of it in exactly those terms, but yes, we are."

"I'm coming with you. In fact, I'm driving. You and your side-kick be ready in five minutes."

He hung up. I looked at David. "Singer wants the pleasure of our company. He's driving us to Galveston."

In four minutes I heard Singer honk the horn on his unmarked car. The audacity of the man — to order us to let him crash our party and then show up a whole minute early!

David followed me out the door. The heat was already stifling. I hadn't worn a tie, and I was glad. Singer looked cool and collected in the front seat of the maroon LTD Crown Victoria. He had the air conditioner on full-blast.

"Gentlemen."

That was the extent of the greeting we received as we got into his car. David was a little nervous about riding in the backseat of a cop car, especially since the back doors don't open from the inside, but I promised to let him out eventually.

"I called Galveston PD and told them I'm going into their jurisdiction to ask some questions for an investigation," Singer said as we turned onto Highway 6. "If we need them, they'll send someone out."

"Good," I said.

It took about twenty-five minutes to reach Galveston and a few more to get to the Yacht Basin. I used the time to tell Singer everything I could about Brian and the problems posed during the past few days. When we reached the Yacht Basin, we parked near where David and I had parked before, and as promised, I let David out of the backseat.

"Where's this boat?" Singer asked.

"Down here," I said, taking the lead. We walked out onto the dock, and I could see the boat about a hundred yards down. Brian wasn't visible; he could be below, or maybe just lying out on the deck. We neared the boat, and Singer came up from behind.

"Which one?" he asked. I pointed.

"Stay back." He went to the boat but didn't board from the dock. He held his 9mm in both hands as he studied the deck. He stood there for much longer than I thought he should have. I thought he would want to call out and order Brian up from the cabin, or go down into the cabin himself, but he did neither. It was minutes later when he said, "Blood."

"What?" I asked.

"One of you get to a phone and call 911. Tell them I said they should get some people out here — cops, ambulance — probably a coroner."

David left without hesitation.

"What do you see?" I asked Singer.

"Nothing yet. A little blood. Not much of it. I'm going below."

Singer got onto the boat, still holding his 9mm. He lifted up the canopy covering the hatch, and the smell reached me almost as soon as it reached him.

"Tell me about this Brian kid," Singer said, looking down into the cabin but not entering. "What's he look like?"

"Sandy hair, good tan, stocky build," I said. "Healthy-looking guy."

"Healthy? Not anymore."

Galveston cops were on the scene within minutes. A thin, short Hispanic detective took over. Singer stood off to the side, just watching the proceedings. From where David and I stood, we couldn't see Brian. Singer said it was probably for the best. A few moments later the small detective approached Singer.

"Your guy has a hole in his chest from a small-caliber weapon," he said. "A few inches left or right, it probably wouldn't have killed him, at least not quickly. But it apparently hit his heart. Bad luck."

"Yeah, bad luck. How long?"

"Don't know yet. More than twenty-four hours probably. But in this heat processes can speed up, so who knows? Anyway, you'll have to come to the station to make a report. Shouldn't take long. These guys with you?"

"Yeah. They knew the victim."

"Not well," I said. "We'd only just met."

"You come too," the cop said. "I'll ride with you."

We walked to Singer's car. This time both David and I were in the backseat. We didn't say anything as we drove a few blocks to the police station on 25th Street. We went in through a back entrance and followed the detective, whose name was Briones, to an office facing the squad room. Singer gave us a commanding look and told us to wait outside the door. The two cops went in. We didn't. We found chairs and sat in the squad room, watching the world pass us by with nightsticks and guns.

A full half hour later Singer emerged. I could hear Briones griping a little. I asked Singer if it was our turn to make a statement. I've always wanted to make a statement. I think I would start off with a statement about my opinion on how the world is run. I would then make another statement, probably about the state of fast-food burritos. I could go on all day, but it wasn't going to be that day.

"No statements," Singer said. "The federal involvement — or noninvolvement — is making this complicated. It looks as if your Israeli commando made one last raid before you caught him."

"Maybe," I said. "That would explain things. But a gunshot in the chest from a small-caliber gun? Would Moshe take a chance like that? He'd more likely put it in your ear, wouldn't he, David?"

"I think so."

That's all David said. We followed Singer back to his car. As we left the building, I asked Singer if the merchandise and the cash had been found.

"Found and impounded."

"Was it hard to find?"

"No," Singer said after a moment. "It was all in a waterproof bag, in a storage locker. Almost in plain sight."

"But if that's why Moshe killed Brian, why didn't Moshe find it and take it back?"

"Good question — one that occurred to me. But it looks as if the State Department wants this closed quickly."

"How about you?" I asked.

"I'd like to see the perpetrator caught, no matter who it was. And, Dunn, it could have been your girl."

"Remington? That's ridiculous."

"Not Remington. Margaret Sullivan."

"She's been with us constantly for the past few days."

"No, Briones was right. He could have been popped last night, after your dinner. She could have snuck out after Remington was asleep, taken Remington's car, and shot her ex-boyfriend. It's been known to happen. I'm going to want to question her."

"I guess that's reasonable. But it couldn't have been her. Obviously Brian wasn't the cream of the crop. He probably had quite a few people upset with him."

"Probably."

We reached the car and got in. Singer didn't say anything else until we reached the newspaper office.

"Dunn, I want to talk to Margaret Sullivan before the day is out."

"She's at Remington's." I gave him the telephone number. "And take it easy on her, Singer. She had a rough night."

"And Brian had a rougher one."

"Yeah, I guess that's right."

I let David out of the backseat again, and we went into the office. The office was almost empty; only Sharon was at her desk. I looked at my watch. It was a little after 1 P.M. My reporters were out reporting or something. David went back to the darkroom to load up on film.

I had a message on my desk; it said to call Maggie. I dialed the number to Remington's apartment. Maggie answered on the first ring.

"This is Emerson. You called?"

"Mordechai wants me to work for him — at his jewelry store. I have experience. What do you think?"

"I think that's great," I said. "He's a good man. You'll like working for him. When do you start?"

"Soon. Tomorrow if I want. A. C. said I could stay with her;

she said she's been thinking about a roommate. Mordechai will come pick me up until I can replace my car."

"That's wonderful," I said. "I wish everything was going that smoothly. Maggie, my dear, the cops want to talk to you."

"What about? They don't still think I stole that money, do they?"

"No, but I think we figured out who did. Brian. But there's a problem — Brian's dead."

She said nothing. It's hard to read silence.

"Maggie, you're going to be getting a call from Bill Singer. You'll remember him from the night your car blew up. He's going to ask some questions, but don't get mad at him. He's just doing what he has to do."

"That's all right. I don't mind. How did Brian die?"

"He was shot."

"When?"

"Yesterday maybe, or last night. They don't know yet."

Again she said nothing.

"Maggie, he's going to call you today. He'll probably want to come by and talk in person. Just answer his questions and you'll be fine."

"All right, Emerson."

"Call me when it's over."

"I will. Good-bye."

She hung up, and I looked over at Sharon, our matronly receptionist.

"What's today?"

"Tuesday," she said.

"Do I usually do any work on Tuesdays?"

"You put out a paper on Tuesday nights."

"Oh, yeah — that. OK. Just asking."

"I made a fresh pot of coffee, Emerson. I might even go get you a cup. You look like you've had a rough week."

"I'd appreciate that."

Nine hours later I was standing beside Louise, pasting up the last of the front-page articles. I was tired, but it was a good edition. Robert had come and gone with his city council story, and Sherri had several good features in the paper. I put the front page in the box with the rest of the finished pages and handed the box to Jimmy, our courier. He would take the pages to the printer and bring back a truckload of newspapers by 6 A.M.

"I'm going home," I told Louise. "I'm beat."

"See you in the morning," she said.

I drove home — again to the new house, which I'd have to officially move into soon. I knew Airborne would be glad to see me. I drove with the windows rolled down. A minor cool front had rolled into the area that afternoon. It was a rare and wonderful thing, with temperatures in the 70s instead of the 90s.

As I drove along the farm-to-market road toward my house, I started thinking about Brian.

What was clear was this: he had stolen the money and drugs and had successfully pinned it on Maggie. She left suddenly and silently, and he saw his opportunity and took advantage of it. He took the money and the coke, then went off to find his lost love. One thing I should have noticed about his story: he told Mordechai that Maggie would be looking for a job, but if she'd just stolen $50,000, why would she need to work? It didn't make sense.

Maybe Brian was trying to kill Maggie because he knew that if she was either dead or never heard from again, no one would doubt that she took the goods.

I passed a new-looking red Ford Escort on the side of the nearly deserted road, about two hundred yards from my house. I looked for a stranded driver but saw none. I put it out of my mind and drove on. I pulled into my driveway and parked. As I emerged from the car I noticed that I'd left the porch light on all day.

I walked to the front door and turned the knob. It was open, as usual. I had a bad habit of leaving it unlocked. I opened the door, expecting to find Airborne waiting for me.

He wasn't. He was sitting on the couch, wagging his tail lazily as Trish raised a pistol in honor of my presence.

"Close the door," she said. Trish was wearing a tight dress. I doubted she had anything conservative. Her high-heeled shoes were in her hand. If it weren't for the gun I would have thought she'd just been relaxing with my dog.

My dog. Airborne Ranger. Some watchdog — he was letting a woman point a gun at me. I thought about how much I paid for him: $35. Worth every cent, I told myself at the time. Now I wanted a refund.

"Where is it? Do the cops have it?"

"Have what?" I asked. Let's see, I bought the stupid dog one ten-pound bag of dog food every two weeks. That comes to twenty-six bags of food per year for three years. That's seventy-eight bags.

"Where's the stuff? Is it still on the boat?"

"No — sorry. The cops took it and put it all in little evidence bags," I said, still standing by the door. "Can I sit down?"

She wasn't paying much attention to me. She was still pointing the gun, but she was thinking hard. I walked slowly to the couch and sat down beside my useless dog. He was chewing on a tennis ball. Let's see, seventy-eight bags of dog food at about $7 per bag — that comes to $546.

"Can you get it?" she asked.

"No, it's in the Galveston Police Department's property room," I said. "And the police station is full of cops. It would be a little tricky."

Not to mention the vet bills. A conservative estimate would be $300 over the last three years.

"How much money do you have?" Trish asked, looking at me with more intensity now.

"You're going to rob me?"

"I've got to get out of here . . . Away."

"I agree," I said. "You're probably in big trouble. Why did you shoot Brian?"

"He wanted her, not me." She left it at that.

"I see." I was beginning to understand. "And he wasn't trying to kill her?"

"Shut up. I've got to think."

She held the gun out with one hand and rubbed her eyes with the other. She stood in the middle of the room, confused and dangerous. She'd probably never spent almost $1,000 on a dog that wouldn't even protect her. And that's not counting the money I spent on tennis balls.

Tennis balls. I had an idea. I reached over and took the ball from between Airborne's front paws. It was a little soggy, but I wasn't going to worry about that. I tossed it up a few inches and caught it with the same hand. I repeated this for a few moments to get Airborne's attention. His tail was wagging, and he was watching the ball intently.

"Trish, I can help you."

"Shut up. Do you have money? Where is it? Where's your wallet?"

It was sort of a dumb question, but who was I to tell her that? Instead I simply rolled the tennis ball onto the floor, between Trish's legs. Airborne bounded off the couch in pursuit of the ball. The hardwood floor was a little slippery for his paws, so when he tried to stop before he ran into Trish, he skidded a bit — straight into her. She went down, and the small automatic went off. I heard a loud "pop," and I saw a mark appear on the floor where the bullet went in. The gun was a little .22 automatic, a woman's gun. It could do some damage at short range, and it could apparently do a number on hardwood floors. I went for her gun hand before she could recover from the fall. I hoped she hadn't broken anything, since it's tough to fall properly when you're wearing an immodest dress. I grabbed her wrists with both hands and put my knee lightly on top of her throat. She released the gun.

"Sorry," I said. "He's a little clumsy yet. But he'll get used to this floor soon."

Airborne began licking Trish's face, as if in apology. His tail was still in motion, so he couldn't have been overly contrite.

I picked up the pistol and recognized it. It was Maggie's. Trish must have lifted it when she visited my apartment. This was the second time a strange woman had pointed that gun at me. I was beginning to think it was a trend I should discourage.

"Trish, I still have a few questions. Now before I dial 911, why don't you explain some things to me."

She didn't respond, so I started trying to put a few things together for myself.

"Brian took off with the money and wanted to find Maggie. But not to kill her, right? To talk her into leaving with him. Into sailing off into the sunset. He was sincere about that. I thought he might have been. But you came looking for her too. You wanted to kill her. So you wired the pipe bomb. Where did you learn that?"

No response. I went back to the couch, still holding the gun. "We could be here all night," I said. "I'm not a cop, so you can tell me. You said you cared about Maggie."

"I care more about Brian," she said, sitting up. She still used the present tense, as if she hadn't recently iced him. "I just wanted to scare her away, at first. The bomb. You think I couldn't do that right? I didn't want to kill her, just frighten her. Moshe taught us about pipe bombs — how to wire them to the car battery and a spark plug."

"Moshe taught you? A woman? I thought he was just training his lieutenants. But then, there are plenty of women in the Israeli army, I guess."

She shrugged. "He taught us to shoot. I could have killed her any time I wanted. I followed you back from Brian's boat, then followed you from your office to here. But I didn't kill anybody."

"Except Brian."

She was silent.

"She didn't want him, Trish. She didn't love him. She wanted to get away, to forget her past. You didn't have to kill Brian."

"I love him."

"So you shot him."

"I don't know what I did. Yeah, I guess I shot him. He told me to get off his boat, that he wanted her, not me. He started pushing me. I was angry."

"I guess you were. Were you angry with me? Would you have shot me?"

"I just knew I had to get out of here. I needed the money, the cocaine. I thought you might know where they were. After I . . . after Brian fell, I got scared and left. I wanted to go back last night. I couldn't. I was working myself up for it today, and I watched the boat. I saw you and the others find Brian. You shouldn't have called the cops. You and I could have shared the money."

"I don't think I'd know what to do with that kind of money, Trish. I'm calling a detective friend of mine. He's going to come arrest you."

She didn't say anything; she just stared at the floor where the bullet went in. I walked to the telephone and dialed. A dispatcher answered. I asked for Singer. He answered.

"This is Dunn. I've got the girl who killed Brian. She also did the bombing and the shootings. Come on over. And, Singer, it's not Maggie."

I hung up and realized that Trish was talking to my dog.

"I wish I were someone else," she said without feeling.

Even with my cockamamie life, I knew who and Whose I was, and that felt very, very good.